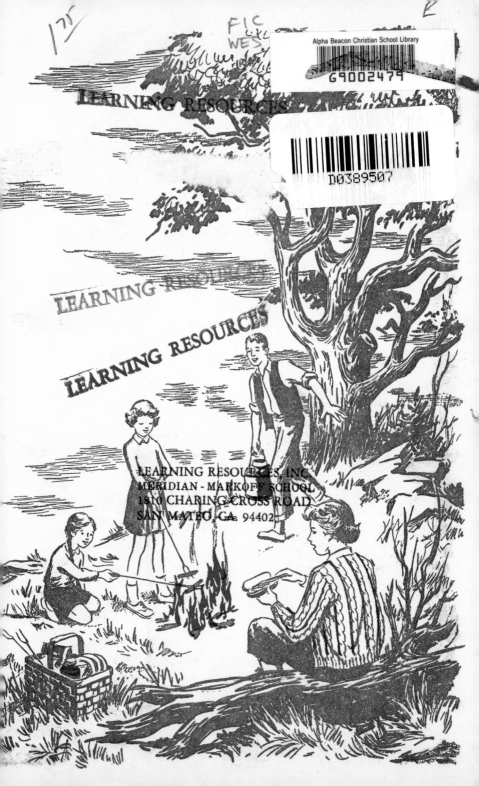

LEARNING RESOURCES

LEARNING RESOURCES

LEARNING RESOURCES

The Happy Hollisters and the Trading Post Mystery

BY JERRY WEST

Illustrated by Helen S. Hamilton

GARDEN CITY, N.Y.

Doubleday & Company, Inc.

Printed in the United States of America

Contents

CHAPTER 1

A Mystery Message

"MOMMY, a telegram boy is coming to the front door!" shouted dark-haired, four-year-old Sue Hollister. Holding her kitten, Cuddly, she ran from the front hall back to the kitchen.

"Hurry!" Sue urged, tugging her mother's hand. "It must be 'portant."

Mrs. Hollister removed a pan of cookies from the oven, followed her skipping daughter, and opened the front door.

"Telegram for Miss Sue Hollister," said the boy. He pulled a yellow envelope from his overcoat pocket.

"For me!" Sue cried.

Mrs. Hollister took the envelope, thanked the messenger, and closed the door against the cold December wind.

"What is it, Mommy?" Sue asked, dancing around.

"Goodness, I can't imagine," her pretty, blue-eyed mother replied. "Suppose you open it."

Sue put her kitten down gently and took the envelope in her chubby hands. She opened it and pulled out the telegram.

"Please read it to me," she said, holding the sheet of paper up to her mother.

A big smile crossed Mrs. Hollister's face as she glanced at it. "It's a telegram from Mr. Vega."

"The out-West Mr. Vega, where we visited last summer?"

"Yes, and do you remember the burro he promised to give you?"

"Domingo?"

"Exactly! Mr. Vega is sending Domingo to you by airplane. He'll arrive at Shoreham Airport tomorrow morning at ten o'clock."

Sue was so excited she shouted and clapped her hands and jumped up and down. Then she stopped and looked straight at her mother.

"It's my very first Christmas present this year!"

"Mr. Vega is sending a donkey to you."

6

When the Hollister family had visited New Mexico several months before, they had stayed with Mr. and Mrs. Vega and their children, Diego and Dolores. The Vegas owned seven burros named for the days of the week. Sue especially loved Domingo, whom she sometimes called Sunday, and Mr. Vega had said she might have him as a gift. But so much time had passed that the children thought he had forgotten about sending the little black donkey.

Sue could hardly wait to tell her brothers and sisters the big news. When she heard children's voices on the back porch, along with the stomping of snowy boots, she hurried to meet Pete, Pam, Ricky, and Holly. A minute later, they burst into the house.

"My you look happy, Sue!" exclaimed ten-year-old Pam.

"Yikes!" chimed in Ricky, who was seven. He removed his ski cap from a mass of red hair and looked at the telegram in Sue's hand. "What's going on?"

"A surprise."

Holly, six, twirled her pigtails expectantly, while her twelve-year-old brother Pete, a cheerful-looking boy with a crew cut, said, "Aw, come on, Sue, what's the big secret?"

"Domingo! We're getting our little burro, Domingo!"

"What?" chorused the others. "When?"

7

"Tomorrow morning," Sue told them, and added that the little donkey would arrive by airplane.

"Oh, boy!" Ricky said. "How are we going to get him home?"

"And where will Domingo sleep?" Pam asked.

"In my bedroom, of course," Sue chirped.

Her brothers and sisters laughed.

"I'm afraid Domingo will have to live outdoors," Mrs. Hollister decided.

"I know!" Pam said. "We'll build a stall for him in the garage. It's certainly big enough."

For the next few minutes, everyone talked at once about the wonderful gift. Finally Mrs. Hollister said, "Pete and Ricky, suppose you figure out how we'll bring Domingo home from the airport, and you girls find a place for him to sleep."

The three girls made their way to the garage, which was set some distance from the Hollisters' big, rambling home on the shore of Pine Lake. Meanwhile, the two boys hopped onto the porch railing and sat down to talk.

"Got any ideas how we're going to bring Domingo here from the airport, Ricky?" Pete asked.

"Seems to me a trailer's what we need," his brother replied.

"That's it! And I know just the one. I saw a pick-up trailer in front of Keck's Service Station the other day," Pete said jubilantly.

"Well, what are we waiting for? Let's go phone him," Ricky suggested, jumping to his feet.

When Mr. Keck, who did all Mr. Hollister's repair work, heard Pete's request, he laughed and said the boys certainly could borrow the truck trailer to carry the burro home.

"I'll call Dad at the store right away," Pete told Ricky. He dialed *The Trading Post*, Mr. Hollister's combination hardware, toy, and sporting-goods store in downtown Shoreham.

In a moment his father answered. "Hello, Dad. We have a big surprise." Pete told his amazed father about Domingo, adding, "And I know how we can get him from the airport." He went on to explain Mr. Keck's generous offer.

"Well, this *is* news," Mr. Hollister said, laughing. "I was just about to leave. Suppose you meet me at Mr. Keck's in ten minutes and help hitch the trailer to our station wagon."

The boys dashed from the house and set off for Keck's. They arrived just as Mr. Hollister pulled in. He was a tall, handsome man with twinkling brown eyes.

They all set to work to attach the trailer in place. Then, after thanking Mr. Keck, the boys and their father drove off. When they pulled into their driveway, Mr. Hollister stopped, and Ricky jumped out to open the garage door. As it rolled up, the boy cried out in surprise.

"Yikes, what's this?"

Blocking the garage doorway was a huge pile

9

of straw. From the center of it Holly and Pam popped up.

"See what we made for the burro!" Holly said. "A bed!"

"We'd better move it out of the way so Dad can put the car in," Ricky said. "Come on, I'll help you."

"Let's make a real stall," Ricky suggested. "I'll get some empty crates from the cellar."

The others helped him carry them out and stack the crates around the straw.

"It really does look like a stall," Pam said. "Oh, I just can't wait to get Domingo!"

The next day, Saturday, the children arose earlier than usual. Before breakfast they went to tell some of their playmates about Domingo. At nine

"We made a bed for the burro!"

o'clock Mr. Hollister, who had gone to open *The Trading Post*, drove back.

The children were waiting, and Mrs. Hollister merely had to put on her storm coat. They rode off.

The roads were rutted from the heavy snow which had fallen a few weeks before, and it took nearly half an hour to reach the airport, located several miles north of town. Mr. Hollister stopped in front of the main building, and Pete and Pam hurried inside to inquire about Flight 322. A young woman behind the counter smiled at the children.

"The plane is on time," she said. "I'd guess from the excitement in your eyes that you must be the children getting the burro." When they nodded, she said, "The pilot radioed us about your pet an hour ago."

Pete and Pam hustled out to tell the others.

While they waited, the children watched several small planes land. Finally Mr. Hollister glanced at his watch.

"One minute to ten," he said. Everyone became silent.

Then Holly whispered, "I think I hear it now."

Sure enough! The whine of an airplane motor became louder and louder.

"There it is!" Ricky cried, spotting the big ship as it circled for a landing.

As the wheels of the huge cargo plane touched the runway, the Hollisters hurried from their car.

11

"Here comes Domingo!"

Pam ran up to an attendant. "May we all go out to get our burro?" she asked.

"As soon as the motors stop," the man replied.

Pam took her two sisters by the hand and they skipped gaily toward the plane. Pete and Ricky dashed ahead of them. By the time Mr. and Mrs. Hollister reached the plane, the copilot was letting a ramp down from the rear.

"Here comes Domingo!" Sue shouted.

"He has a red ribbon around his neck!" Pam exclaimed.

As the little black donkey, saddled and bridled, set his feet on the runway, the children rushed up to hug him. He seemed to remember them and brayed loudly. Pete noticed that a note was attached to the ribbon on the burro's neck.

"It's poetry!" He read aloud:

"Bed me down at Christmastide
And I with you will long ——!
Y.I.F."

"What does that mean?" Sue asked her father.

"I don't know," he said. "Do you children remember anything the Vegas said that might be a clue?"

All shook their heads, and Pam remarked, "What rhymes with 'Christmastide'?"

"Ride, hide, sighed, abide," said Pete.

"*Abide*. That's it!" said Ricky. "'Bed me down at Christmastide and I with you will long abide.'"

"Now if we only knew who Y.I.F. is," Pam sighed.

Sue rode the burro to the trailer and two airport attendants helped Mr. Hollister and his sons lead

Pete read the mysterious note.

Domingo onto it. They tied his halter to a metal loop. Domingo seemed very alarmed by all these strange happenings and tried to pull away. Pete decided to ride along with him in the trailer. The boy's friendly presence seemed to calm the little animal.

The other children took their places in the station wagon and watched Domingo out the rear window while Mr. Hollister drove home. When they got there, everyone got out, and Pete untied Domingo. As he gazed at his new surroundings and Pete took off the bridle and saddle, Zip, the Hollisters' collie, ran up. The two animals rubbed noses.

"They're friends!" Sue cried delightedly.

Just then three other children came running down the driveway. "Oh, he's nifty!" cried a tall, twelve-year-old boy. He was Dave Mead, a friend of Pete's.

Behind him were Jeff and Ann Hunter, who lived down the street. Gray-eyed, dark-haired Ann was ten and her brother was eight.

"What fun!" Ann exclaimed, patting the friendly burro.

"Where are you going to keep him?" Dave asked.

"We made a stall in the garage. Come see it," Pete said.

As they led Domingo into his homemade stall, another voice cried out, "What you got? Lemme look!"

Joey slapped Domingo.

Pam sighed. Joey Brill! He was a mean boy Pete's age and in his class at Lincoln School. The broad-shouldered, husky fellow had made trouble for the Hollisters ever since they had moved to Shoreham. Now, Joey elbowed his way past the other children into the garage.

"That's a dumb-looking horse," he said, sneering.

"It's not a horse," Sue corrected. "It's a burro!"

Without warning, Joey slapped Domingo on the flank and gave a loud cry. The burro, frightened, bolted from the garage. Free, he ran through the yard and raced headlong toward the shore of frozen Pine Lake.

"Domingo's running away!" Sue wailed.

CHAPTER 2

Hunting a Santa Claus

Poor Domingo! The little burro was so confused he did not know which way to run!

Reaching the lake front, he raced along the shore for a few yards, then turned into the Smiths' back yard. All the children except Joey Brill joined in the chase. Dave Mead caught Domingo by his ribbon bow but only succeeded in untying it. The burro dodged him.

"Stop! Please, stop!" Pam shouted.

But Domingo merely raised his head and went on.

"He's headed for Sunfish Cove!" Ricky panted. He hoped one of the skaters would catch Domingo.

As the frightened animal crashed through some bushes, he found himself looking straight at several skaters. Seeing him, they started to laugh and point. This seemed to startle Domingo. Before he could decide what to do next, Pete rushed up from behind and grabbed the red ribbon.

"There, boy," Pete said soothingly. "Nobody's going to hurt you."

Soon all the children who had chased him and many of the skaters crowded around.

"He's a swell pet."

"Say, he's keen."

"Where'd you get him?"

"What's his name?" several asked.

Some of the Hollisters' other school friends waved at them from the shiny ice, and one boy shouted for Pete to bring the burro down. Pam carefully led the animal down a little slope to the lakeside, where a number of youngsters were warming their hands around a small bonfire.

"He's a swell pet!" a boy named Ken said admiringly.

"I don't think so!" came a shrill voice.

Everyone turned to see Will Wilson, one of Joey Brill's friends. Will, who was oversized for his age, always sided with Joey against the Hollisters. Now he made a face as he approached on his skates.

17

"Let's pin the tail on the donkey!" he said, grabbing Domingo's tail.

"Let go of him!" Holly scolded.

"Okay, I'll pull your pigtails instead!" the big boy teased.

But he did not come any closer, for one look from Pete convinced Will that he had better not try it. As Will skated off, he tried to do a figure eight, lost his balance and fell flat on the ice. Everyone laughed, loudest of all Ricky.

Will picked himself up red-faced. Angry, he shouted, "I still say he's a mangy old burro!"

"He is not!" Ricky defended the Hollisters' pet. "He's the best burro in the whole country."

"If he's so good," taunted Will, "let's see him skate!"

Holly held her head high. "He can skate!" she bragged.

"Ha! Well, what are you waiting for? Let's see him skate, then," Will Wilson said.

"I'm sorry," Pam said, stepping forward. "We can't put skates on Domingo. He might fall."

"Then you're afraid," Will taunted the Hollisters.

"Yes, I'm afraid of hurting our burro," Pam replied firmly. "Nobody should harm animals."

"Who can hurt that dumb old critter?" the boy scowled. "Here, I can tie my skates on his front feet."

As Will approached Domingo, Pete reached out and grabbed his arm. "Stay away from our burro!" he warned the bully. One glance convinced Will that Pete meant what he said.

"Okay!" Will retorted, trying to laugh. "Can't you take a joke?"

Just then several children standing near by started to giggle, but not at Will Wilson. They were watching Ricky and Holly, who had borrowed two pairs of skates and were attaching them to Ricky's hands and feet.

"Ricky, what are you doing that for?" Pam burst out.

"I'm going to ice skate on all fours instead of Domingo," he replied with a grin. "Ee-aw, ee-aw!" Ricky bent over and made his arms and legs go up and down like a donkey. As the onlookers howled,

He tried to imitate a donkey.

he slipped and slid over the ice, finally falling on his stomach.

"Oof!" the redhead exclaimed. "I'm glad we didn't put the skates on poor Domingo. Look what happened to me!"

Pete and Pam helped their brother up and unfastened the skates from his hands.

"Come on," Pete said. "It's time to go home."

The children led Domingo back to their garage, put him in his stall, and fed him some oats. But before they went into the house, Sue pulled the animal's head down close to hers and whispered in his ear, "Won't you please tell me who 'Y.I.F.' is —the one that put the note on my Domingo?"

At the dinner table that night, Ricky's ice skating adventure was repeated. Mr. Hollister laughed. Then he, in turn, began to talk about the Christmas decorations he was using at The Trading Post.

"We have wreaths and other decorations," Mr. Hollister said, "but still the place lacks something. Have you any suggestions?"

"I know what your store needs, Dad," Pam said. "A big make-believe Santa Claus with his sleigh and reindeer. You could put it on the roof of The Trading Post."

Mr. Hollister raised his eyebrows in surprise, then said, "Hmmm, that sounds like a good plan."

"We could fill the sleigh with toys for poor children," Holly added.

The thought of having Santa Claus and his reindeer on the roof of the one-story *Trading Post* building excited all the youngsters.

Suddenly Pete snapped his fingers. "Dad, how about selling cheaper than the regular price any toys that people might want to give to poor children?"

Pam clapped her hands. "We could deliver them Christmas Eve!"

"And be Santa Claus's helpers!" Holly said excitedly.

"All your ideas are fine," Mr. Hollister agreed. "But first we would have to find Santa Claus, his sleigh and reindeer. Let's call Indy Roades, and then check with Tinker at the store to see if they know where we might buy a complete outfit."

Tinker was the kind old man whom Mr. Hollister had employed when he opened *The Trading Post*. Indy Roades also worked at the store. He was an Indian who had come from New Mexico.

"Please let me phone them!" Ricky begged.

"All right."

Ricky hurried to the telephone, dialed Indy's number, and eagerly waited. Ricky loved Indy and his dog, Blackie. They had been good friends ever since the Hollister children had untied a tin can from the dog's tail after a mean boy put it on.

"Hello, Indy," Ricky said when the man answered.

He quickly explained what the Hollisters wanted to do at *The Trading Post* and asked Indy if he

"Dad, you'd better talk to the man."

knew anybody who sold Santa Clauses, sleighs, and reindeer.

"Well, that's quite an order," the Indian said. "I'm afraid I don't know anyone in that business. But Tinker has lived in Shoreham all his life. Suppose you call him."

Ricky said he would do this and hung up. Then he telephoned Tinker. The elderly man was at once interested in the plan.

"Yes, I know somebody who makes models like that," he said. "The man lives in Clareton. His name's Greer. But he's usually sold out of Santa Claus equipment by this time."

"We'll try him, anyway," said Ricky.

He thanked Tinker, then told his family about Mr. Greer. Pam picked up the telephone book and looked in the Clareton section. Sure enough, there was a Mr. Greer, listed as a model-maker.

"I'd better talk with him," Mr. Hollister said, and his daughter gave him the number.

All the children waited eagerly while their father spoke to Mr. Greer.

"You say you have just one left?" he asked. "Yes, yes, fine! Tomorrow, early in the afternoon. Good-by."

"Yikes!" Ricky shouted, and all the children besieged their father with questions.

"How big is the Santa Claus?"

"How many reindeer?"

"Can we keep it for good?"

Mr. Hollister laughed. "I can't answer a single one of your questions. But you'll find out tomorrow." Mr. Hollister turned to his wife. "Elaine, what say we all drive out there after dinner tomorrow?"

"Fine," Mrs. Hollister agreed. Then she put her arms around Sue and Holly, saying, "Time for you two little girls to go to bed—and Ricky, too."

It was the custom in the Hollister home for Pam and Pete to stay up a little later than the others.

"Let's go see if Domingo's all right, Pete," Pam suggested.

They turned on the garage light and hurried outside. The children could hear a thumping noise and found their new pet kicking at the door. He

Domingo had knocked over his stall.

had knocked over his stall made of crates and scattered the straw.

"Why Domingo!" Pam exclaimed.

"I guess he doesn't like it in here," said Pete, starting to fix the stall. "Listen, boy, you'll just have to get used to things away from the ranch," he told the little donkey.

Suddenly Pam had an idea. "Dolores told me burros get lonesome," she said. "That's probably what's the matter with him. Why don't we bring Zip out here to keep Domingo company?"

"But Zip's our house watchdog at night," Pete reminded his sister.

"That's right. Then how about Cuddly and her mother? And the rest of the kittens?" Cuddly's mother was named White Nose.

Pam ran back to the house to bring the cat and

her five babies out to the garage to keep Domingo company. How delighted the burro seemed to see them! He lay down on the straw contentedly with White Nose and her family.

On the way back to the house, Pam said, "We'd better write to Mr. Vega for Sue and thank him for Domingo."

"Let's do it right now," Pete said, opening the door.

Pam had written thank-you notes before. As she sat down at the desk, Pete said, "Be sure to ask Mr. Vega if he knows about the mysterious verse we found on Domingo's ribbon."

Pam wrote a neat, newsy letter and signed the names of all the Hollister children. By the time she had sealed the envelope and stamped it, Pete appeared with his jacket on.

"I'll mail it at the box on the corner," he said, and hurried out of the house.

When Pete returned a few minutes later, he heard the telephone ringing. Pam was already on her way to answer it.

"Hello," the girl said. Pete paused to learn who the caller was. He saw his sister's face grow pale.

"Who is it?" he asked, worried.

Pam put down the receiver and turned to her brother, a frightened look in her eyes.

"Pete!" she blurted, nearly in tears. "We can't keep Domingo!"

CHAPTER 3

An Antler Ride

"WHO says we can't keep our burro?" Pete asked Pam in surprise.

At this moment Mr. and Mrs. Hollister came downstairs. "What's this you're saying?" Mr. Hollister demanded.

"The—the Board of Health says we can't keep Domingo!" Pam wailed.

"What!" cried Mr. Hollister unbelievingly. "Who told you this?"

"The man said he was head of the Board of Health."

"Mr. Stone?"

"He didn't give his name, Dad."

Mr. Hollister said that Mr. Stone, a customer of his, was chairman of the Board of Health. In a few minutes Mr. Hollister had him on the wire.

"No, I didn't telephone your home," Mr. Stone said. "And I know nothing about your burro. People in Shoreham can't keep horses unless they have a special kind of stable. But the law doesn't cover burros," he said laughingly. "I'll ask the other members of my board, however, if any of them phoned your house. I'll call you back."

As Mr. Hollister was about to say good-by, Mr.

Stone added, "It's very strange that two people should have called me in such a short time about the stable ordinance."

"What do you mean?" Mr. Hollister asked.

Mr. Stone explained that a boy had called him a short time before. "Maybe he has a new pony," the man remarked and hung up.

When Mr. Hollister told Pete and Pam about the query from a boy, Pete snapped his fingers and exclaimed, "I'll bet that was Joey Brill! He's trying another one of his mean tricks on us!"

"Now don't worry about this until we hear more," Mrs. Hollister said, putting her arms on her children's shoulders.

A few minutes later Mr. Stone telephoned. He said none of the Board members had called the Hollisters and, furthermore, it was all right for them to keep the burro.

"You won't have to put him in a special stable, either."

"Then we can keep him in our garage?"

"Yes, you may, Mr. Hollister, and I hope your children have lots of fun with him. Good-by."

The following day was a bright, clear Sunday, and the children were awakened by the sound of church bells. They found Domingo happy and frisky when they fed him. And each child had a ride.

The family went to service and had an early dinner. Then they set out for Clareton. It was a small town, and Mr. Hollister had no trouble finding Mr. Greer's home.

As the children scampered out of the station wagon, Sue spied a man walking from the back of the house toward a big barn in the rear. She raced up the driveway to him and said, "We came to buy a Santa Claus."

The man looked down at her and smiled. "I'm sorry, little girl, but they're all gone," he said. "I sold the last one yesterday."

Sue's mouth puckered up and tears began to roll down her pink cheeks. Then, bursting out crying, she turned and ran toward her mother, who was walking up the driveway.

"Somebody bought our Santa!" she wailed.

Hearing this, the man turned around and went

"We came to buy a Santa Claus."

to greet his callers. When Mr. Hollister identified himself, Mr. Greer said, "Oh, for goodness sake, I didn't know you were the Happy Hollisters. I certainly made your little girl unhappy. Indeed I do have your Santa Claus. Come with me."

"Where do you keep your Santa Clauses, Mr. Greer?" Ricky asked.

"In the barn where I make them," he answered, opening the door.

As the Hollisters stepped inside, they saw a sleigh hitched to eight reindeer. On the seat sat a jolly fat man wearing a red suit and cap.

"Is—is that Santa Claus?" Holly asked, puzzled.

The figure in the sleigh had a kind face indeed, but if it were Santa, Holly thought, someone had shaved off his beautiful whiskers!

Mr. Greer chuckled. He stepped to the barn door and called toward his house, "Emmy, Emmy, will you please bring the whiskers and some glue?"

"You see," Mr. Greer said to the children, "I don't put Santa's whiskers on until he is ready to leave here."

"Why?" Sue asked.

"Because the barn swallows like to make nests in the whiskers," Mr. Greer said, and the Hollisters laughed.

It did not take long for the man to glue the whiskers onto the apple-cheeked Santa Claus figure.

He glued the whiskers on Santa Claus.

"Now he looks real!" Holly said.

Mr. Hollister was very pleased with the whole outfit. "This is exactly what I had in mind for *The Trading Post*," he said, smiling.

There was a twinkle in Mr. Greer's eyes as he told the others to watch him. He pulled a long extension cord from under the sled and asked Pete to insert the plug into a wall socket. The boy did this.

Instantly the lead reindeer's nose lighted up, all the heads began to turn from side to side and the jolly song "Jingle Bells" started to play.

"Yikes!" Ricky said, hopping up and down gleefully. "This is super!"

"The best one I've ever seen!" Mrs. Hollister commented.

"I thought you'd like it," Mr. Greer chuckled.

"I'll pick it up in my truck tomorrow," Mr. Hollister said.

As the two men talked a few minutes, the children walked round and round the reindeer and sleigh. They climbed in and out, pretending to drive. Sue asked Ricky to hold her up so she could see what made the reindeer's necks turn. The boy held her as high as he could next to one of the reindeer's heads. Sue giggled as the nose turned one way, then the other, nearly touching her own.

As she put up her arm to pat him, suddenly one of the antlers caught the collar of her snow suit. The little girl was pulled from her brother's arms. Sue swung helplessly in the air as the animal's head moved from side to side!

"Help! Help!" she cried.

Mr. Hollister sprang toward the little girl. Just as he reached her, the reindeer let go and Sue fell *plop* into his arms.

"Oh, Daddy, I didn't like that kind of a ride," she said, hugging him tightly.

"Well, I guess we've seen enough for today," Mr. Hollister remarked. "We'll go now."

While he made final arrangements for picking up the Santa Claus display, the others started for the car, talking excitedly about their new possession.

Soon the family was on its way home. Mr. Hollister took a different route, and as they passed a

31

roadside farmhouse, Pam read aloud a large sign which said:

"STOP HERE!
CUT YOUR OWN CHRISTMAS TREE!"

"Wouldn't that be fun, Dad?" Pam said. "Please let's stop."

Mr. Hollister agreed and backed the car up several feet to the lane which led into the farmhouse.

"Oh, boy, may we really cut our own Christmas tree?" Ricky cried excitedly.

Off to the left of the house was a grove of beautiful bushy evergreens of various sizes and varieties. A man in high boots was walking among them, attaching tags here and there.

When the car stopped, the Hollisters got out and approached him. He told them his name was Quist.

"Here's a beauty."

"Pick out the one you want, children," Mr. Hollister said.

"Here's a beauty," Pete called, pointing.

"Yes, that is a nice one," his mother agreed, looking at the well-shaped balsam. "But it's rather short, isn't it, Pete?"

"Guess you're right, Mother."

Suddenly from a distance came a squeal of delight. Everyone turned to see Holly jumping up and down in great excitement.

"Oh, look what I've found!" she exclaimed. "Come quickly!"

As they reached Holly's side, she pointed high into the bushy branches of a tall, stately spruce.

"See! Up there! A real bird's-nest," she said. "Oh, please, let's choose this tree."

"The tree *is* a beauty," Mr. Hollister agreed. "But what would you do with the nest, Holly?"

"I know just the place for it, Daddy," she explained. "I'll take it to school and Miss Tucker can put it in our nature exhibit. I'll be the first one to find a bird's-nest for it!"

"How about it, children? How many votes do I hear for Holly's bird's-nest tree?" Mr. Hollister laughed.

Everyone was in agreement that Holly had found just the right tree for their home, and when they asked Mr. Quist if the nest went with the tree, he said jovially, "Why sure. 'Finders keepers.'

Holly reached for her treasured nest.

You may have it, little lady. Here," he said, "I'll hoist you up. You can take the nest now and come back for your tree later."

High in the air in the hands of the sturdy farmer, Holly reached for her treasured nest. Holding it gently in one hand, she was lowered to the ground.

The farmer handed a tag to Mr. Hollister, saying, "Write your name and address on this, please, and tie it to the tree trunk."

"We'll come back a few days before Christmas," Mr. Hollister promised, "and cut down the tree."

"Crickets! Look!" Pete cried out. "Rabbit tracks."

"Let's follow 'em," Ricky suggested. "Boy, this will be fun!"

"I want to come, too," said Pam.

The three dodged in and out among the trees to follow the tracks which went in a zigzag course through the grove. As the pawprints grew further apart, Pete whistled.

"This rabbit was really hopping!" he said.

"I see him!" Pam called. "There he goes!"

At the top of a little rise ahead sat a pure white rabbit. He took one look at the children and leaped away, his white tail disappearing over the brow of the hill.

"Come on! Let's catch him!" Ricky shouted.

They ran from the Christmas tree grove into a stubbly cornfield alongside which ran a stream. The rabbit scampered across the frozen brook and hid himself in some brush on the other side.

"We'll surround him," Ricky said excitedly.

"I'm not sure the ice will hold us," said Pam.

But the boys did not want to give up the chase.

"The brook looks as if it's frozen solid," Pete replied. "I'll try it."

Leading the way, he stepped out gingerly onto the snow-covered icy crust of the brook. It held him and he went on.

"It's okay. Follow me!" he said.

But he had hardly spoken when crunch, the ice cracked. Before Pete could run to shore, the ice gave way and he dropped into the water!

CHAPTER 4

Two Bullies

As PETE crashed through the ice, Pam and Ricky screamed. They did not know how deep the stream was and feared their brother would go in over his head.

The cold water took Pete's breath away. Fortunately, when his feet touched the bottom of the stream, he was standing only chest high in the water.

"Don't worry," he called to his sister and brother. "I can get out of this easily."

Pete rested his elbows on the ice and tried to wriggle up out of the hole. But the ice around him kept cracking off. Twice he nearly made it but slipped back again each time. By this time he was numb from the cold and his teeth were chattering.

"We'll help you," Pam offered, becoming worried.

A moment later Mr. Hollister appeared. He had heard the children scream.

"Oh, Dad, help us get Pete!" Pam begged.

Their father ran to the edge of the brook. He lay down on his stomach and inched his way toward Pete. Finally their hands touched.

"Grab on and hold tight," Mr. Hollister di-

He pulled Pete from the icy water.

rected Pete, then said to the other children, "Hold my feet in case the ice cracks under me."

Ricky held onto one of Mr. Hollister's shoes while Pam grasped the other. They tugged frantically and slowly pulled their father backwards. He in turn pulled Pete from the icy water, inch by inch. Finally the boy, too, lay flat on the ice and was drawn to the shore.

Pete shivered as he rose to his feet. "Wow, I'm cold!"

Mr. Hollister said there was not a second to lose. "You must get to Mr. Quist's house at once. Try to run all the way, Pete, before the water freezes on you."

They all set off at a brisk pace.

"I—I guess I'm all right. My toes were numb for a while, but I can feel them again," Pete panted as they neared the small farmhouse.

Mrs. Hollister, followed by Holly and Sue, hurried toward the dripping boy. They were quickly told the story and went with Pete to the house. The front door swung open, and Mrs. Quist said, "Oh, dear, what happened?" Upon hearing of the accident, she said, "You poor boy! Hurry in!"

She led Pete into her warm kitchen and gave him a chair alongside a wood stove. Quickly she and Mrs. Hollister bent down to remove Pete's boots and mittens. Then they massaged his feet and hands until warmth came back into them.

Presently Mr. Quist came in. Hearing what had happened, he said to his wife, "Ebba, I'll take this boy upstairs for a change of clothes."

Pete, his trousers clinging to his skin, followed the man up a narrow stairway. A few minutes later, the boy reappeared, wearing a red and white bathrobe that reached to his ankles and was much too large.

Mrs. Quist laughed. "You look like our Christmas *Jul-Nisse* coming out of the attic," she said.

"*Jul-Nisse?* What is that?" Holly asked.

"Oh, he belongs to all the Scandinavian countries," Mrs. Quist explained. "Papa and I are Danes. Although we have been in the United States a long time, we still remember Christmas as it was back in Denmark."

"Please tell us about *Jul-Nisse*," Pam begged.

Mrs. Quist brushed back a wisp of blonde hair from her forehead and waited until her husband had hung Pete's clothes back of the stove to dry.

Then she said, "The *Jul-Nisse* is as mysterious as Santa Claus is. We know about him, but we never see him."

The children listened eagerly while the kind Danish woman told them that the *Jul-Nisse* was a very sweet little old man who lived in one's attic. He was seen by nobody but the family cat.

"Whenever strange things happen in the house," Mrs. Quist said, shaking her finger, "we believe the *Jul-Nisse* has done it. But he is a good fellow. He makes sure that the animals on the farm are taken care of."

Mr. Quist nodded. "The *Jul-Nisse* sees to it that they are always watered, tended, and bedded."

His wife went on with her story. "Every Christmas Eve," she said, "the children in Denmark put

She told them about the Jul-Nisse.

39

a bowl of porridge and a pitcher of milk at the entrance to their attics. And next morning, guess what?"

"It's gone!" Ricky said.

"Yes, it always is," Mrs. Quist replied, laughing.

"The *Jul-Nisse* eats it?" Holly asked.

When Mrs. Quist nodded, Sue hopped over and sat in her lap. "Does the *Jul-Nisse* have a mother?" the little girl asked.

"I never heard of one."

"Then who feeds Mr. *Jul-Nisse* the rest of the year?" Sue asked, perplexed. "He must get awful hungry."

The woman shrugged. "And you children must be hungry, too," Mrs. Quist said without answering Sue's question. "Especially you, Pete. Are you getting warm?"

The boy had stopped shivering. He admitted that he was hungry.

She hurried to the pantry for milk and chocolate. In a few minutes, the delightful aroma of steaming chocolate filled the kitchen. Everybody had a cupful. Then Mr. Quist passed around a plateful of crisp Danish cookies.

"Yum-meee, these are good," Ricky said, taking a drink of chocolate.

By the time the Hollisters had finished eating, Pete's clothes were dry. He went upstairs to put them on, returning in a few minutes. The Hollisters bundled themselves into their warm coats and thanked their kind hosts.

"When you come back for your tree," Mrs. Quist said, "stop in and see me."

"Thank you, we'd like to," Mrs. Hollister replied.

"Good-by," Sue said, waving. "I'm going home and look for the *Jul-Nisse* in our attic."

The Hollisters sang Christmas carols all the way home. Holly, holding the bird's-nest in her lap so as not to crush it, added a song about wintertime birds. She could hardly wait for the next day to come so she could carry the nest to school.

After breakfast next morning, Mrs. Hollister said to her, "I think you'd better put it in a bag, dear."

"Oh, Mommy, I want to show the nest to all my friends on the way to school," Holly pleaded. "May I, please?"

"All right, but be sure not to drop it," her mother said. "Birds'-nests are very fragile."

The four children left for school together. Sue was not yet old enough to go, but she constantly talked about kindergarten and played school at home. Holly and Pam hurried ahead while Pete and Ricky stopped at their garage to put some grain in Domingo's box.

"He looks kind of lonesome," Ricky remarked. He patted the burro and said, "I'll play with you after school."

Meanwhile, Holly and Pam were far ahead. Sud-

41

denly Holly looked up at her sister and said, "Do you suppose the *Jul-Nisse* put that funny note on Domingo's ribbon?"

Pam smiled. "Why do you think so?" she asked.

"Because the verse was signed Y. I. F., and *Jul-Nisse* begins with a Y, doesn't it, Pam?"

"No, honey, with a *J*."

"Oh, dear," said Holly. "When are we ever going to find out?"

Pam was assuring her sister they would some time, when Joey Brill and Will Wilson ran up to the two girls.

"Hey, what you got there?" Will asked, seeing the bird's-nest.

"Trying to be teacher's pet, taking something to her, huh!" Joey sneered.

The girls did not answer. Joey and Will edged closer.

"Want a better look, Will?" Joey said, winking at his friend.

As if by accident, Will hit the underside of Holly's arm and the bird's-nest flew backward into the air.

"Stop that!" came a voice behind them as Ricky ran up.

He was just in time to catch the nest before it hit the ground. He handed the nest back to Holly.

"Oh, a good catcher, eh?" Joey taunted Ricky. Then he added, "Say, Will, suppose you and I play ball with the nest."

"You can't have it!" Holly cried, pulling away from him.

As he reached toward the girl, Pam pushed the bully. Joey shoved her back.

"Quit it!" Ricky cried out, thumping Joey on the chest.

"Don't get wise!" Joey shouted, pushing Ricky toward Will Wilson. Will gave the little boy another shove and Ricky fell to the ground.

Just then there came the sound of running feet. Joey turned around and shouted, "Hey, Will, look out!"

But the warning came too late. Pete Hollister made a flying leap at Will, knocked him flat on the ground and fell on top of him.

"You can't have this nest!"

Ricky jumped around excitedly. "Serves you right, Joey, for pretending you were the Board of Health and saying we couldn't keep our burro!" he shouted.

"That was only for fun," Joey cried before he realized he was making a confession.

Will struggled to his feet, and for a few moments he and Joey both punched at Pete, who finally landed a direct hit on Joey's cheek. Suddenly a siren sounded and a car pulled up to the curb.

"Run! It's a cop!" one of the onlookers shouted. But before anyone had a chance to break away, a handsome young policeman stepped from his car and hurried over to the boys.

"Officer Cal!" Pam said.

The Hollisters knew Cal Newberry because they had helped him solve a mystery shortly after their arrival in Shoreham.

"Why can't you fellows play together peacefully?" the policeman asked.

"Okay, we will," Will said, looking very pouty.

"Now, all three of you shake hands," the officer continued.

The boys did this without much enthusiasm, and Cal watched them as they made their way into the schoolyard before driving off.

"We were lucky," said Holly as she left the others and hurried to her classroom. "Joey might have ruined my prize."

Her teacher, Miss Tucker, was delighted with the bird's-nest and said it had been made by a wren. All the children looked at it as they told the story of the Christmas tree.

"And now, Holly, will you please place the nest in the nature exhibit?" Miss Tucker requested. Holly proudly placed it in the glass case at the back of the room.

Then the children marched to the auditorium for assembly. Principal Russell announced that the school would have a pageant the Thursday before Christmas, depicting holiday customs in other lands.

"Each class will represent a different country and will work out its own skits," he said.

Holly's first-grade class was assigned Switzerland. Ricky's second-graders were to do Norway. Pam's fifth grade had Italy, and Pete's seventh-grade room was to depict the Netherlands.

Plans were begun at once, and the Hollisters hoped to be given various parts. What a busy, exciting day it was for them! And to end it, Mr. Hollister was to bring the sleigh and reindeer to be put on the roof of The Trading Post.

The children eagerly watched for their father at suppertime, but he did not come. They finally ate. Still he did not arrive.

"Do you suppose anything is the matter?" Pam asked her mother nervously.

CHAPTER 5

Funny Masks

JUST as the children and their mother were growing fearful that Mr. Hollister might have had an accident, they heard the horn of his truck *beep* in the driveway.

"Daddy's here! Daddy's here!" Sue shouted.

She and the others made a dash for their coats and hats and ran out the back door to meet him. How glad they were to find he was all right!

And what a funny scene they saw lighted up by the big floodlight over the garage door. In the back of the truck was Santa Claus seated in his sleigh, but the reindeer were not pulling it. Instead, they were piled all around him as if they had dropped from the sky. One of the wooden deer was lying in the sleigh, and the two front feet of another were hanging over the truck's tailboard.

Standing in the driveway beside the truck were Mr. Hollister and Indy Roades.

"Hello!" the Indian said. Then with a laugh he added, "We just arrived from the North Pole!"

"Oh, is that why you took so long?" Holly asked.

"We thought you'd never get home," said Pam. "Did something happen?"

"Yes, it did," Mr. Hollister replied. "Come into the house and I'll tell you about it."

Sue took Indy's hand as they walked inside. "You tell us, too," she said.

Indy, shorter than Mr. Hollister, had broad, athletic-looking shoulders. He had a kind face and a fine smile. While he and the others took off their coats, Mrs. Hollister set a place at the table for him. He and Mr. Hollister began to eat and to tell what had delayed them so long.

"We nearly lost the Santa Claus," Mr. Hollister said. "Herman Tash was the cause of it."

Pete's eyes widened. "The man who runs the hardware store a block away from *The Trading Post?*"

"The same one," Indy put in. "He wanted the Santa Claus, too. Claimed he had bought it."

Mr. Hollister explained that Mr. Tash had ordered a Santa Claus and reindeer the spring before, but in September he had sent Mr. Greer a letter canceling his order.

"And then he changed his mind again?" Pam asked.

"He must have," Mr. Hollister said, "because when we arrived with the truck, Mr. Tash was in front of the barn arguing with Mr. Greer. Mr. Tash insisted that our Santa Claus belonged to him."

"But there was nothing he could do about it,"

47

"Ee-aw! Ee-aw!"

Indy said. "Finally, Mr. Tash stopped arguing and went off in his car. But he was very angry."

Ricky heaved a great sigh. "I hope he'll leave our Santa alone. When are we going to put everything on top of *The Trading Post*, Dad?"

"Tomorrow."

"Will you wait 'til we're out of school so we can help you?" Holly asked.

"Sure thing. You children come directly from school to the store. I'd like your help."

Next morning the Hollister children were up as early as usual because all of them had jobs to do. The boys fed Domingo. Then, wanting to have some fun, they led him to the back porch, lifted him up, and poked his head into the kitchen.

"Ee-aw! Ee-aw!" the burro brayed.

The three girls burst out laughing, and Pam gave him a lump of sugar.

"Good morning to you!" she said.

Holly had just given Zip some breakfast, but he looked up from his dish on the floor to give several sharp barks. White Nose was waiting for her food and began to meow loudly. Once more Domingo said, "Ee-aw! Ee-aw!"

What a din there was!

"Gracious!" Mrs. Hollister exclaimed. "Take that burro back to the garage!"

Things quieted down again, and an hour later the children started for school.

That morning Holly's class was to study about Christmas customs in Switzerland. Miss Tucker read to the children from a picture book.

"The day they have the most fun," she said, "is December fifth. That's when they celebrate Saint Nicholas day. He's their Santa Claus, and is called *Samichlaus.*

"To welcome him the children parade through the village streets," the teacher went on. "Sometimes the part of *Samichlaus* is played by a little boy. He wears a crimson fur-trimmed robe, a red jovial-looking mask and a long white beard. He has many attendants and followers. All the children wear gay masks."

"That must be fun," Holly said.

"And there is a special surprise for the girls," Miss Tucker added. "Along with *Samichlaus* comes

"Meet Samichlaus."

a beautiful maiden named Lucy. She hands out gifts to all the good little girls in the village."

"And not the boys?" a lad back of Holly asked.

"I'm afraid not," Miss Tucker said. "Now we shall plan our part in the school pageant. We'll need a boy to play *Samichlaus* and a girl to play the part of Lucy."

"Oh, I want to be chosen," cried several children, including Holly.

Miss Tucker smiled. "We'll put all the girls' names in one hat and all the boys' in another."

Two girls sitting near the cloakroom dashed into it for their hats. The pupils wrote their own names on little pieces of white paper. When all the slips were in the right hats, Miss Tucker pulled out a boy's name first.

"Ned Quinn," she said. He was a friend of Ricky's.

The children clapped, and the blond-haired boy, laughing, took a bow and said, "Meet *Samichlaus*."

"And now," Miss Tucker said, "the first name I pick out of the girls' hat will be Lucy."

Everyone became quiet, and Holly's pulses were pounding with excitement. She would so love to be chosen for the part!

Slowly Miss Tucker pulled out a paper and unfolded it.

"Who is it? Who is it?" several girls shouted.

"Lucy is—Holly Hollister," Miss Tucker announced.

"Oh, she'll made a wonderful Lucy!" Donna Martin said as all the pupils cheered.

"What do we do next, Miss Tucker?" asked Donna.

"Let's make masks," the teacher said.

Donna, who had brown eyes and hair and plump, rosy cheeks, slipped into the seat alongside Holly as Miss Tucker passed out colored paper and scissors.

The teacher propped the picture book up on her desk so the children could see what the masks looked like. Soon the sound of snipping scissors filled the room.

"Oh, Donna, I have a real silly one," Holly giggled. "How does it look on me?"

Donna laughed out loud. "You look like a Halloween pumpkin with a crooked nose. How does mine look?"

"Like a sad pussycat that's been crying," Holly answered, putting her hand across her mouth to keep from laughing.

By this time, all the children had completed their masks. Miss Tucker showed them how to connect elastic bands to the sides so that the masks could be held securely about their heads.

"Now we'll have a parade, like the children in Switzerland," she said.

The boys and girls adjusted their funny masks and started marching around the room. Holly's mask kept slipping down so she could not see where she was going.

Bang!

She sat down kerplunk.

Ricky and Holly mounted the ladder first.

Holly hit her head hard on the edge of the door which had just been opened by Principal Russell. She sat down *kerplunk* on the floor.

"Oh, dear!" Miss Tucker cried out, hurrying over. Mr. Russell was already helping Holly to her feet and saying how sorry he was.

"I—I saw stars!" the little girl remarked.

"You poor child!" the teacher said, taking off the mask and examining Holly's forehead. "You're getting a lump on your head. Come, we'll put cold water on it."

She led Holly to the drinking fountain in the hall and soaked her handkerchief. Holly held it to her forehead and soon felt much better. By the time the closing bell rang, she had forgotten all about it.

The four Hollisters met and hurried to their father's store. Indy said Santa, his sleigh, and the reindeer were waiting to be hoisted to the roof. Each piece would be lifted up separately, and the outfit put together later.

"All set with the ropes to hoist Santa and the other things up?" Mr. Hollister asked Indy.

"Everything's ready," the Indian replied.

He had fastened a stout board to the roof of the one-story building. To the end of it was attached a pulley and a rope dangled through this to the sidewalk.

"What can we do, Dad?" Pete asked, as Indy climbed the ladder to the roof.

Mr. Hollister said the children might follow Indy and help put Santa Claus, the sleigh and reindeer into position. Ricky and Holly mounted the ladder first to the snow-covered roof. Then Pete and Pam followed. There was a wide ledge around the roof. However, Indy cautioned the children not to lean over too far.

"We'll be careful," Pam promised.

On the sidewalk Mr. Hollister was busy tying one of the reindeer to the end of the rope. A crowd had already gathered to watch the proceedings.

"Say, this is going to be nifty," a red-haired boy exclaimed.

"A wonderful idea," said a man coming out of the store.

"It really looks like Christmas now," a woman

Santa came up next.

remarked. "Santa Claus has come to Shoreham."

When the reindeer was tied securely, Mr. Hollister hoisted it to the roof. Indy leaned out and grabbed one of the reindeer's legs. The children helped him pull it over and stand it up. The operation was repeated until all the wooden animals were on the roof.

By this time the crowd below had grown so large that it extended across the street.

"We want Santa Claus!" the red-haired boy shouted. "Send him up!"

"Santa's last," Mr. Hollister replied, chuckling. He fastened the sleigh at both ends, then slowly pulled on the rope. Up, up it went.

"I have it!" Indy called down, as he and the children grabbed the sides of the sleigh and set it alongside the reindeer.

Santa was next. Mr. Hollister tied a rope around the bewhiskered man's red coat and the jolly figure followed the sleigh to the roof as the crowd cheered. When all the pieces were in place, Indy and Pete fastened them together with wire so that the wind could not blow them over.

"That's a good job," the Indian told the children. "Thanks for your help."

Pete was eager to see how everything looked from across the street. Quickly he climbed down, followed by the others.

"It sure does look good, doesn't it?" he said to his father, pleased at the way Santa Claus had been rigged up.

But Mr. Hollister was not paying attention. His eyes were searching the crowd in front of the store.

"Where's Ricky?" he asked. "Didn't he come down with you children?"

"I didn't notice," Pam said. She glanced about but Ricky was nowhere in sight.

"He must be on the roof, Dad," Pete suggested. He cupped his hands and called up, "Hey, Rick! Rick! Come on down!"

There was no reply. Pete quickly climbed the ladder and looked around the roof. Ricky was not there. When Pete came down again and reported this, Pam became frightened.

"Dad," she said in alarm, "you don't think Ricky could have fallen off the building, do you?"

CHAPTER 6

Another Strange Note

WHEN Pam expressed her fear that Ricky might have fallen off the building, everybody became worried. The crowd was silent as the Hollisters began a search.

Pete hurried down an alley on one side of the building while Pam raced along the other. Mr. Hollister and Holly ran through *The Trading Post* to the rear. Still Ricky could not be found!

When the searchers returned to the street, Will Wilson, who was in the crowd, called to Pete, "Say, I bet I know where your brother went!"

"You do? Where?" Pete asked eagerly.

"I think I saw him running home, crying," Will said.

"What would he do that for?" Pete asked, not certain whether to believe Will or not.

"No reason. He's just a big crybaby!" Will said.

"He is not!" Holly defended her brother, as Pete turned away in disgust.

Suddenly Pam cried out, "Listen, everybody!"

The sound of a deep chuckle could be heard. "Ho, ho, ho! Merry Christmas, everybody!"

The voice seemed to come from the rooftop, and everyone looked up. The bag on Santa Claus's back wriggled a little and suddenly a boy's head popped out of it.

"Ricky!" Holly shrieked. "He's been hiding in Santa's bag."

"Merry Christmas! Merry Christmas!" Ricky called out again.

"Same to you!" cried several in the crowd.

Mr. Hollister, much relieved, shook his head over the boy's prank. "Come down here," he ordered. "We've all been worried about you."

Ricky climbed down the ladder and Indy put it away. Dusk was beginning to fall and Pete said, "Dad, it's time to turn on the lights, isn't it?"

Mr. Hollister, looking up at the darkening sky, agreed. "Okay, click the switch, son," he replied.

Indy had put the plug into an extension cord which led to the inside of The Trading Post. When Pete flipped the switch, a floodlight showed up the scene. The lead reindeer's nose lighted up, the animals turned their heads from side to side and the air was filled with the strains of "Jingle Bells." The onlookers clapped, and some began to hum the familiar Christmas tune.

"Those Hollisters certainly have happy ideas," said a gray-haired woman.

"Oh, they're not so great," a boy grumbled under his breath. He was Joey Brill.

He bent over and made a hard snowball. Taking careful aim from behind a telephone pole he let it whizz toward the roof of The Trading Post.

Pete dashed after Joey.

Smack!

The snowball hit the lead reindeer on the nose. *Crash* went the red bulb, scattering into a thousand pieces.

"Who did it?" Pete shouted angrily.

"That boy who is running away," the woman volunteered. "What a mean thing to do!"

Pete caught sight of Joey and dashed after him. But Joey turned the corner and disappeared.

"I'll settle that score later!" Pete declared.

As he returned to the store, Holly hurried up to him. "Indy put a new bulb in. See, the reindeer's nose is working all right again."

Pete glanced up to see the new light in the reindeer's swaying head.

"Joey'd better not break this one," he said.

At this moment Dave Mead, who had just arrived, hurried over to the Hollister children.

"The outfit up there sure is swell," he said. "There's never been anything like it in Shoreham."

Ricky told him about Joey, and Dave said, "He's just trying to get even, I'll bet."

"What do you mean?" Pete asked quickly.

"Oh, haven't you heard?"

"Heard what?"

"Guess who's delivering orders for Mr. Tash?"

"Not Joey Brill!"

"Yes."

"So that's why he threw the snowball at our Santa Claus outfit," Pete said. He told Dave about how the hardware store owner, Mr. Tash, had tried to buy the sleigh and reindeer that had been promised to the Hollisters.

"Joey's probably sore because your store got it," Dave said. He laughed. "You'd better keep an eye on him. He may try to knock Santa's head off next time!"

"You're right," Pete said. "I'm going over to Mr. Tash's right now and speak to Joey if he's there."

Accompanied by Dave, Pete walked to the next street and into Mr. Tash's store. It was far from neat, and a variety of items were scattered in untidy piles all over the floor. Joey was at a counter wrapping an order as Pete approached him. He scowled when he saw the two boys.

"What are you doing here?" Joey asked sullenly.

"I'm here to warn you about our Santa Claus outfit," Pete said. "Don't throw any more snowballs at it!"

"I'll throw snowballs any time I feel like it," Joey snapped back.

"I'm warning you for the last time," Pete said, and left the store.

Arriving back at *The Trading Post*, he found his father, sisters, and brother ready to leave for home. Dave went with them as far as his house, then said good-by.

At home Sue was excited to hear about the reindeer and wanted to see them, so Mr. Hollister drove her downtown to see the display.

"Oh, Daddy!" she cried in delight. "Your store is the mostest, bestest one in town!"

"And I hope," he said, chuckling, "that it will bring the mostest, bestest gifts to the unfortunate children who may not receive any special presents."

"I hope the sleigh has so many things in it, they'll reach to the sky!" Sue said, clapping her hands.

By the time she and her daddy reached home, supper was ready.

"Crickets, it's getting cold!" Pete said, as an icy blast of wind rumpled his hair.

They went into the garage and patted the burro. Suddenly Ricky shouted, "Look at this, Pete! Another note on Domingo!"

Around the burro's neck was a ribbon similar to the one they had found before. On it was a message which read:

"I'm the best little burro in creation.
Please use me for a Christmas ——."
Y.I.F.

"Yikes!" said Ricky. "What rhymes with creation?"

"This one's easy," said Pete, grinning. "I'll bet it's *decoration*."

"You mean we should hang Domingo on the Christmas tree?"

Pete laughed. "Try and do it! But maybe he could be a decoration in some other way."

Ricky sighed. "If Domingo could only talk, he could tell us who this mysterious Y.I.F. is!"

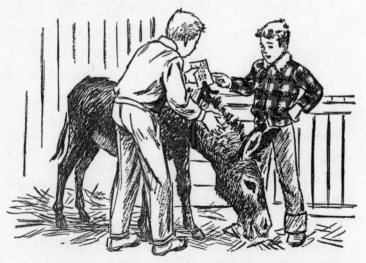

"If only Domingo could tell who Y.I.F. is!"

Just then the burro went "Ee-aw! Ee-aw!" and the boys laughed.

Then Ricky sobered. "Pete, doesn't Dad say 'yours sincerely' on business letters?"

"Yes. Why?"

"I'll bet Y.I.F. stands for 'yours internally forever.'"

Pete roared. "You mean eternally, not internally, Ricky. But even if you are right, it doesn't tell us the writer's name."

"I guess you're right," said Ricky. "Anyway, Mr. Vega couldn't have written this note. But who was it?"

Pete put the note into his pocket to show to the other Hollisters later. Then he got a bucket of grain for the pet while his brother brought a pail of fresh water. Domingo tried to follow them outside.

"He missed his exercise today because we didn't come right home from school," Pete said. "Come on, old boy, I'll give you a run."

He climbed onto Domingo's back without bothering to put on the saddle, and away they went! Soon Pete regretted that he was riding bareback.

"Hey, Domingo, take it easy!"

But the little donkey was having too good a time to stop and raced down the street as fast as he could go with Pete clinging to his stubbly mane.

Pam asked Pete to listen to her ad.

"Whoa! Whoa!" the boy cried.

Finally Domingo turned back. How glad his rider was to get off! Pete limped into the house and put a pillow on a chair before sitting down to study his homework.

He showed the note he had just found on the donkey to his family. Mr. Hollister stroked his chin.

"This really is a mystery," he said. "It's Domingo's secret all right."

"But we'll solve it," Pam declared, as she got her schoolbooks. When she finished studying, she said to her father, "Dad, have you put an ad in the newspaper yet telling people they can buy gifts for the sleigh at a special price?"

"No, Pam, I haven't. How would you like to write one for me tonight?"

"Okay, Dad," Pam replied. "First, I'm going to listen to Pete's spelling words."

Pete and Pam often helped each other with their homework, Pam listening to her brother's spelling, and Pete checking his sister's arithmetic problems.

When this was done, Pam sat down to write an advertisement. She asked Pete to listen to it.

BE A SANTA CLAUS

. . . like the one on the roof of *The Trading Post!*

Help fill our sleigh with gifts for people less fortunate than you!

The Trading Post will grant a special low price on presents for the sleigh.

All items will be gift-wrapped and delivered by us on Christmas Eve.

When Pam finished, Pete exclaimed, "That's swell, Pam. Let's show Dad."

They hurried into the living room, where Mr. Hollister was reading the evening paper, and showed it to him.

"This is fine!" he said. "A good job, Pam. Suppose you leave it at the office of the *Shoreham Eagle* tomorrow morning."

Pete and Pam left the house early for school in order to make the stop. As Pete had guessed the evening before, it had grown very cold, and at

They chased around in circles.

times the two children had to walk backward against the wind. The result was that Pete smashed squarely into a tree!

"Oh, the poor maple!" Pam teased, and Pete grinned.

They went on and soon reached the *Eagle* office.

"Look who's here," Pam said.

In front of them at the classified ad counter stood Joey Brill. He had a piece of paper in his hand and was saying to a young woman:

"Mr. Tash wants you to put this ad for a Santa Claus outfit in tomorrow's paper."

Then he turned around. His eyes widened when he saw the Hollister children.

"Oh, trailing me, eh?" Joey said unpleasantly. "Always trying to play detective." Then he sneered, "You're not going to get away with what you're doing!"

66

"Get away with what?" said Pete.

"Well, Mr. Tash is going to get a Santa Claus —and a sleigh and reindeer, too. And they're going to be twice as large as yours!"

With that Joey pushed open the street door and hurried out.

"I'll bet he doesn't find another one!" Pete said as he handed the advertisement to the clerk.

But Pam continued to worry about the affair, although her brother forgot about it during school hours.

As the Hollister children met after school that afternoon, Pete said, "Let's go skating. The ice is swell."

Ricky readily agreed, and the two boys hurried for their skates. Soon they were gliding over the glassy surface, making figure-eights and chasing around in circles.

Pam and Holly stopped for a few minutes at the Hunters' house. When they finally reached their own home, they were just in time to meet Sue who came running from the garage.

"Pam! Holly!" she shouted as she raced up to them. "Something is terrible wrong with Domingo!"

"What do you mean?" her sisters asked fearfully.

"Domingo—he—he's shaking all over!" Sue cried out.

CHAPTER 7

A Balky Burro

WHEN Pam and Holly heard that Domingo was shaking, they ran to the garage. Sue, meanwhile, hurried into the house to bring her mother.

Pam reached Domingo first. The sad-eyed burro was huddled in the straw, shaking convulsively.

"Oh, you poor thing!" Pam cried, kneeling down and putting her arms around the little animal. "Are you sick?"

"Maybe he has a tummyache," Holly suggested, stroking the pet. "We'll get you some burro medicine, Domingo. Pam, what kind of medicine do you suppose burros take?"

"I don't know. We'd better ask a horse doctor."

At this moment Mrs. Hollister rushed in with Sue. Leaning over, she felt Domingo's nose. Giving a sigh of relief, she said, "Thank goodness, he's not ill. His nose is cool and moist. There's nothing the matter with him except that he's cold!" She stroked the shivering animal. "He's not used to such low temperatures where he comes from."

"Let's pile some blankets on him," Sue suggested. "I'll get the one off my bed, Mommy."

68

"Maybe I have an old one in the attic," Mrs. Hollister said.

"Mother," Pam said, "why don't we make a blanket coat for Domingo to wear?"

"Excellent!" Mrs. Hollister replied. "And I have just the thing for it. An old automobile robe."

She said her parents had used it many years before when cars did not have heaters in them. It was still in good condition and very warm.

Mrs. Hollister and her daughters hurried into the house and up to the attic. They found the old robe in a mothproof bag.

When Pam took it out she exclaimed, "It's pretty. Domingo will look nice in a woolly plaid coat."

They returned to the first floor and cleared the dining-room table so they could use it to work on.

"Domingo will look nice in a plaid coat."

Holly went for the big scissors, and Pam returned to the garage with a tape measure to get the burro's size.

Quickly she stretched the tape from his neck to his tail. "Thirty-eight inches," she said. "And he's thirty-six around his neck. Oh, and around his tummy he's—let's see—sixty inches."

Pam patted the burro, saying, "You'll soon be warm," and went back to the dining room.

Mrs. Hollister said that the blanket was just large enough to make a coat to fit around Domingo's chest and cover his sides and flank right to his tail.

"Get me two long pieces of tape and two buckles," Mrs. Hollister asked Holly. These would be sewed on to hold the blanket in place and would fasten under the neck and just behind the front legs.

By this time Mrs. Hollister had the material cut to the right pattern. Pam and Holly took turns sewing on the tapes to hold the buckles. Suddenly they missed Sue. When the little girl did not answer her mother's call, Pam called out, "Sue! Susie-baby!" She knew her little sister did not like to be called a baby, and if she were anywhere within hearing, she would certainly object. But there was not a sound.

Holly ran to the kitchen window and looked out. "There she goes into the garage, Mother. She's probably going to keep Domingo happy while we finish his coat."

"Domingo was nearly froz-ded."

Mrs. Hollister and the two girls went on working. A few moments later they heard a clippety-clop, clippety-clop on the back porch. The kitchen door flew open.

Clippety-clop, clippety-clop!

"What is that noise?" Mrs. Hollister gasped as she laid the scissors down on the woolly material.

She rushed to the kitchen, followed by Pam and Holly. There in the middle of the floor stood Domingo with Sue holding onto his halter!

"Gracious!" Mrs. Hollister exclaimed. "Sue, you shouldn't have done this. Look at the floor. It's all scratched!"

"I—I couldn't let poor Domingo freeze out there," the little girl replied, peering up from under her ski cap. "He was nearly froz-ded. Now he'll stay nice and warm 'til we put his coat on him."

Pam and Holly burst into giggles. Soon Mrs. Hollister was giggling, too. What a funny sight it was to see Domingo sniffing the shiny white refrigerator.

"Maybe he's hungry," said Sue, and gave him a carrot from the refrigerator. "Please, Mommy, let him stay here."

"All right, Sue. We'll hurry and finish his blanket. You watch Domingo."

As the three hurried back to the dining room, Pam said, "Domingo's coat should have a name on it."

"And bells," Holly added.

She dashed up to her room and returned with a handful of tiny silver bells. With needle and thread she attached them to the corners of the burro's overcoat. How prettily they tinkled!

Pam cut out the letters D-O-M-I-N-G-O from an old yellow skirt and sewed them onto the side of the coat. Now it was ready to try on the burro. But as Mrs. Hollister, Pam, and Holly went into the kitchen with the blanket in their arms they heard a *plop.* Domingo had decided to sit down!

"Get up!" Sue ordered. "Your new overcoat's ready to try on." But the burro merely looked her straight in the eye and did not move.

"Look, it's a new coat to keep you warm!" Holly said. "Come on, Domingo. Be a good burro and get up on your feet."

The donkey just sat.

Pam said nothing but disappeared into the pantry and returned with a lump of sugar. She held it in front of Domingo's nose. He nibbled it contentedly, but would not budge. The three girls pushed and hauled, but the little donkey remained where he was.

"Goodness!" Mrs. Hollister said. "How are we ever going to get him out of here? It's time I started supper."

Sue put her hands on her hips and wagged her head. "I guess Domingo will have to have supper with us."

As Pam and Holly laughed, Ricky and Pete rushed in.

"Crickets, this is crazy!" Pete said, laughing.

"How'd he get here?" Ricky exclaimed, wrinkling his freckled nose.

Mrs. Hollister said they were trying to get the burro to stand up.

"I know one thing he'll have to stand up for," Ricky said.

With that he burst into the national anthem. Pete and the Hollister girls stood at attention. The donkey did not seem to understand. He just sat.

"Huh," Ricky said, scratching his head.

"I know what will work," Pete spoke up, and hurried out of the house.

He returned in a few minutes with an automobile jack his father used to hoist the car when he changed tires on the station wagon. But every time Pete tried to get the jack underneath Domingo, it slipped on the polished linoleum.

"Well," Mrs. Hollister said, heaving a sigh, "I guess we'll have to give up."

No sooner had she said this than Domingo, making a loud clatter with his hoofs, stood up.

"Hooray, hooray!" Ricky shouted.

"He was only teasing us," Pam said. "Come on, Mother, quick. We'll try his coat on now."

The blanket overcoat was thrown across the burro's back and Mrs. Hollister buckled it underneath.

"Doesn't he look gorgeous?" Pam chuckled.

"Maybe we could put him in a burro fashion show," Holly snickered.

Sue showed him Domingo's overcoat.

Everyone laughed, then Mrs. Hollister said, "Suppose you boys take him back to the garage."

"This way!" Ricky said, taking the burro's halter.

Domingo followed, and a few moments later was back in his homemade stall. The boys gave him his supper and also fixed meat and milk for White Nose and her family.

While Mrs. Hollister began supper preparations, the girls cleaned up the dining room. By the time their father arrived home, the room was neat and the table set.

Sue took her father out to show him Domingo's overcoat. "That's fine," her father remarked. When they returned to the house, he said, "My family is always doing nice things to make others happy."

"Everybody should be happy, shouldn't they,

Mommy?" Sue said, looking up at her mother, who was in the midst of broiling a large steak.

"You not only made Domingo happy, but you made me happy today, too," Mr. Hollister went on mysteriously.

"How, Daddy?" Pam asked.

Mr. Hollister said that the idea of selling toys at a low price for the gift sleigh was catching on like wildfire.

"Even before the ad comes out in the newspaper," he said, "people have started coming in to the store and purchasing gifts for the needy. I have a whole pile of boxes stacked in Santa's sleigh already."

"Oh, goody!" Holly said, clapping her hands. "But Daddy, what will happen to them if it snows?"

Mr. Hollister lifted the lid on a simmering pot of lima beans and sniffed the sweet aroma.

"Ummm. Oh, yes, that's a good thought. I suppose we ought to keep something on hand to cover the gifts, just in case it should snow again before Christmas."

Pete offered his camping poncho which was in the garage. "Let's put it over the gifts tonight," he said.

Mr. Hollister agreed, and after supper the whole family set off in the station wagon. As they neared the store, Ricky cried out, "Yikes, look at the crowd!"

People were looking up at the reindeer and chuckling over the red nose of the lead animal and the bobbing heads. Mr. Hollister parked the car. They climbed out and he unlocked the front door of *The Trading Post*. Pete hurried to the rear for a ladder, and with his father and Ricky helping, carried it out the back door.

Ricky held the poncho while Pete placed the ladder against the side of the building. Suddenly in the bright light he caught sight of two parallel lines scraped on the bricks.

"Say, Dad, look at these funny marks!" he called.

Mr. Hollister examined them. "Ladder marks," he said. "But we didn't put our ladder here last time."

"Here's something else, too!" Ricky shouted. "See these footprints."

Somebody with big feet apparently had tried to put a ladder against the building, and it had slipped down.

"The person may have been frightened off," Mr. Hollister said.

Suddenly a look of alarm came into Pam's eyes. "Dad," she exclaimed, "do you suppose someone was trying to get on the roof to steal the gifts out of Santa's sleigh?"

CHAPTER 8

The Runaway Cart

"PLEASE, Dad, see if any of the gifts were stolen from the sleigh," Pam begged as she looked up at the Santa Claus on the roof of *The Trading Post.*

"Indeed, I will," Mr. Hollister said.

After setting the ladder firmly in place, he climbed up. Pete followed, carrying the poncho.

"Is anything gone?" he asked as his father finished counting the brightly colored gift boxes, tied with gay ribbons of all colors.

"No, I'm glad to say. Nothing has been touched." He called the good news down to Pam.

"Someone could have been planning to, though," Pete said. "Wouldn't it be safer to keep the gifts in the store?"

Mr. Hollister said he felt that Shoreham had such good police protection no one would dare climb onto the roof and steal the Christmas packages.

"Besides," he continued, as Pete spread his poncho over the gifts and tucked it in, "I understand that the police patrol this street constantly every night."

Relieved to hear this, Pete followed his father down the ladder, then returned it to the store. As they drove home, Sue snuggled against her mother and fell fast asleep. When they reached home, Mr. Hollister carried his littlest daughter up to her bedroom. She was undressed without waking, and did not open her eyes again that night.

Meanwhile, Ricky had found a notice of a telegram which had been attached to the front doorknob. His father at once telephoned the office about it and learned the message was from Mr. Vega.

"KNOW NOTHING ABOUT NOTE TIED ON BURRO. LET ME KNOW ANSWER WHEN YOU SOLVE MYSTERY. GREETINGS TO ALL INCLUDING DOMINGO."

"Huh!" said Ricky. "Now we'll have to start all over again." He cupped his chin in his hands. "Who could Y.I.F. be?"

"I have an idea," said Pam suddenly. "Maybe the pilot or someone else on the cargo plane did it. Let's call up the airport and find out."

Mr. Hollister made the call and talked with an official of the airline. The man checked the names of all those working for the company, but not one of them had the initials Y.I.F.

"Oh, dear," Pam sighed. "How can we ever find out?"

Next morning Ricky was up early to clean Domingo's stall and feed the burro before leaving for school. He also wanted to be alone with him because the boy was secretly teaching the little donkey to do some tricks.

Ricky made a long chain.

"Shake hands," he ordered and Domingo obediently put up his right front hoof. For this he received an apple.

Next Ricky held the burro's head between his hands and swung it from side to side, all the while saying, "Do two and two make five?" Then he let go and repeated the question. Domingo merely stared.

"Oh, dear," Ricky said. "Well, I'll give you another lesson after school. You have to have all your tricks ready by Christmas."

At school that day Ricky's teacher said they would make chains of colored paper for the school's big tree to be used in the Christmas pageant. She gave the children little jars of white paste and scissors.

"You may start right away," Miss Berry said.

Ricky's eyes twinkled. He loved to dabble in paste. For a while he worked carefully and made a long string of red, green, and yellow circles.

"And now we'll make some paper lanterns for the tree," the teacher said. She made one, then added, "This is the way you paste the handle onto the top of the lantern." She fastened a thin strip of paper to the top.

Ricky made one, then he decided to tie a long chain onto the lantern.

"But I need more paste," he told himself. "I'll get some from Jimmy." He was the boy sitting behind him.

Ricky turned quickly and leaned over just as Jimmy lifted his paste jar.

Squish! Ricky's turned-up, freckled nose went right into the jar!

"Oops!" Jimmy exclaimed. He burst out laughing at the gooey sight.

All the children looked around as Ricky touched his nose. Now his fingers were white, too. When the other youngsters saw this, they giggled.

This made Ricky feel silly. He picked up his Christmas chain and pasted it on the tip of his nose.

"Look at me! I'm a Christmas tree!" he said, and everyone, including the teacher, laughed.

"You'd better go wash your face and hands," she said and Ricky went to do this. When he returned, Miss Berry was saying, "And now I want to talk about decorations and gifts for some unfortunate people."

She explained that a very poor family lived not far from the school. Wouldn't it be nice to make up a Christmas basket of food for them? All the children agreed, and Miss Berry suggested that they bring money which they would earn themselves if their parents agreed to the idea. The pupils clapped their hands and said they would like to earn the money.

"I know how I'll raise some," Ricky said. "With our burro Domingo. Maybe my brother will help me build a cart, and we could deliver orders from my dad's store. I'll bring the money we earn to you, Miss Smith."

"Hey, Dave! Want to help build a cart?"

Jimmy Cox and the other children thought this was a keen idea, much better than shoveling snow or washing dishes to earn money.

On the way home from school, Ricky talked the idea over with Pete.

"That's super!" his brother said. "Hey, Dave!" he called to his friend, who was passing by. "Ricky and I are going to make a cart for our burro. Want to help us find the parts?"

"Sure," Dave replied eagerly. "Say, there are two old carriage wheels and an axle in the barn back of our house. They're kind of rusty, but I think they'll do."

"Swell," Ricky said.

When the Hollister girls heard the plan, they wanted to help, too. At once Holly said, "I saw part of an old pony cart down in Donna Martin's cellar. Maybe her mother will let us use it."

They ran over to Donna's and spoke to her about it. The little girl went upstairs for her mother, who came down at once.

"Yes, you may borrow the cart top," she told the Hollisters. "I used it when I was a little girl. I'm sorry the wheels are gone."

"We have some," Ricky said quickly. "Come on, fellows, let's get the cart."

All the children trooped down cellar to see it. The four-foot wicker body with facing seats and an opening at the back was just what they wanted, Pete declared. The boys lugged it out to the back yard, then went off for the carriage wheels and axle in Dave's barn. They found them under an old hayloft, lying beside a big rake.

"Yikes!" said Ricky. "They're neat!"

Some harness hung on a nail above the wheels. "Maybe you could use this, too," Dave offered as he pulled it down and blew off the dust.

"Sure," said Pete.

The two wheels were still in good condition, even though rusted and cobwebby. And they looked a bit big for the cart top, but this made no difference to the Hollisters, who rolled them out of the barn and over to Donna's house. Dave followed with a wrench, screw driver, hammer, bolts, and screws.

Turning the cart top over, Pete examined the wooden floor and decided that the best place for the axle was a foot from the front. He forgot entirely that there should be proper balance.

When the axle was attached, it stuck out beyond each side about a foot. And after the oversize wheels were set on, they lifted the cart a little higher than it was supposed to be.

"It's funny, but it's nice," Holly remarked.

Proudly Pete got between the shafts and trundled the cart to the Hollister driveway, followed by the other children.

"I'll get Domingo," Pam offered.

She held the burro while her brothers put on the harness. When he was hitched to the cart, the

Pete got between the shafts.

basket tilted badly toward the front. No one cared about how odd this looked, though.

Ricky wanted the first ride, but Pete said, "Pam, you try it."

She let the burro go, but before she could climb the step into the cart, Zip came bounding up to them. With one great leap he landed in ahead of her.

"I guess Zip wants to be the first rider!" Holly chuckled.

But the children's smiles quickly turned to looks of alarm as Domingo, frightened by Zip's leap, bolted down the driveway. As the children chased him, calling for Domingo to stop, they were surprised to see that Zip stayed inside the cart. The collie looked unconcerned as Domingo raced into the street and headed toward town.

"Stop, Domingo, stop!" the Hollisters kept shouting, but the burro seemed determined to give Zip a good ride.

Suddenly a car came toward the cart and the children held their breaths. The burro veered off to the right, but one wheel of the cart hit the curb. A second later the bolt came loose and the wheel flew off. The cart stopped abruptly. As the wheel jumped over the sidewalk, Zip leaped out to chase it. The wheel rolled rapidly across the lawns of several houses.

Pete and Dave, fast runners, raced off to catch the wheel before it struck something or someone. But it had too much of a head start.

Suddenly Pete shouted, "Dave, look!"

The wheel skidded on a patch of snow, changed its course and sped directly toward the glassed-in porch of a beautiful white house.

Holly held both hands over her eyes and shrieked. The wheel was sure to crash through the lovely window! To make matters worse, there was a gentle slope in the lawn and instead of stopping, the wheel began to roll faster.

Zip seemed to think this was great fun. He cavorted along beside the rolling cart wheel, barking happily.

In a split second, Pam, who had almost caught up to the boys, had an idea. "Zip! Zip!" she shouted. "Stop that wheel! Get it, boy!"

CHAPTER 9

Ricky's Delivery Service

WHEN Pam shouted for Zip to stop the rolling wheel, the collie's ears went up instantly. He seemed to understand exactly what the girl meant.

With a bound the dog flung himself against it. The wheel quivered for a moment, then *plop*, it fell to the ground, only inches from the glassed-in porch.

"Zip's a hero!" Holly cried, dancing toward him.

"Phew!" Pete exclaimed as he pulled off his ski cap with one hand and wiped his forehead with the other. "That was close!"

"Too close!" Dave agreed. "Boy, what a smart dog!"

As Zip sniffed at the rim of the wheel, the other Hollisters ran up, including Sue. She burst into tears.

"Our nice wagon is brok-ded!" she wailed.

As the tears streaked down her cheeks, a smiling woman opened the front door of the white house. The children recognized her as Mrs. Wallace.

"I saw what happened," she said. "Your dog did a good deed, and I'm going to give him a reward."

She went for a giant-size dog biscuit shaped like a bone, and Zip took it gratefully.

"My goodness, what are you crying about?" the kind lady said to Sue. "You're the Happy Hollisters, aren't you? Happy people don't cry!" She laughed. "Anyway, if you don't dry those tears, they'll form icicles on the end of your nose," she teased.

When Sue heard this she began to giggle.

"I hope you'll be able to repair your cart," their neighbor went on.

After Mrs. Wallace had gone inside, Pete and Dave picked up the wheel and rolled it back to the cart. Ricky had located the loose bolt and screwed it on while Domingo stood patiently waiting to set off again.

Zip jumped back into the cart, and Pam led the burro home. Pete found a big wrench and made the bolt very tight.

"Now the wheels won't come off," he said, and Sue and Pam clapped delightedly.

The children played with the cart until dusk, taking turns riding in pairs down the block in it. As Pete and Pam were coming into the driveway, Mr. Hollister arrived. He laughed heartily upon seeing the strange contraption.

"It's a pretty good outfit," he said, "but I'm afraid it's a little hard on Domingo. Better unhitch him."

Holly grabbed her father's hand. "Before we do, won't you sit in the cart and try it?"

Mr. Hollister put one foot on the step at the

The burro dangled crazily.

rear of the cart and pulled himself up. Instantly the body tilted backward and poor Domingo was lifted off the ground!

The burro dangled crazily in the air. He began to kick frantically and bray loudly. Even when Mr. Hollister stepped down and the frightened animal felt the earth under his feet again, he continued to cry "Ee-aw, Ee-aw."

Holly and Sue rushed over to comfort him. They hugged and patted the little animal until he quieted down. Now the Hollisters could laugh.

"Crickets, I wish we could have had a picture of Domingo, the flying burro," said Pete.

At supper Ricky told his father how he wanted to earn some money to give a poor family Christmas baskets by delivering orders for *The Trading Post*. "May I, please?"

"All right, but you'd better bring Pam with you. Come down after school tomorrow."

The following day turned out to be a half-holiday in the Shoreham schools because of teachers' meetings. Directly after lunch Ricky and Pam hitched Domingo to the cart, and Pam drove to *The Trading Post.* The store was crowded with Christmas shoppers.

"Tinker put your packages over there," Mr. Hollister told his son, pointing to the rear of the store. "The names and addresses are on them."

Pam helped her brother load the packages into the cart.

"Here's one that isn't marked," she said.

"I'll ask Tinker about it," Ricky offered and went to find the kindly, gray-haired man.

"Oh, the tall carton?" Tinker said. "That's an ironing board for Mrs. Ritter, 16 Beech Street."

Ricky hurried back and carried the carton to the cart which was parked back of the store. Domingo set off at a merry pace along the main street of Shoreham. People stopped to wave at the two children, and automobiles went *beep, beep* in salute.

"Let's go to Mrs. Ritter's and get rid of the big carton," Ricky suggested.

A few minutes later they pulled up in front of 16 Beech Street. Ricky lifted the long, awkward package out of the cart and carried it up the walk to the front door. When he rang the bell, a gray-haired woman answered.

"Here's your ironing board from *The Trading Post*, Mrs. Ritter," Ricky said importantly.

"Oh, thank you, young man," the woman replied. Then she added, "Aren't you rather young to be delivering such large orders?"

When Ricky explained that he and his sister were earning money toward a Christmas basket for a poor family, Mrs. Ritter smiled and said, "Here, maybe this will help." She pressed a fifty-cent piece into Ricky's hand.

He thanked her and skipped happily back to the cart. He climbed in opposite his sister and said, "Look what Mrs. Ritter gave us—a whole half-a-dollar. We've made some money already."

"That's wonderful," Pam agreed. Then, lifting the reins, she said, "Giddap!"

"What a large order!"

The burro had taken only two steps when suddenly Mrs. Ritter threw open her front door and called out, "Little boy, there's been a mistake!"

Ricky was a little frightened, but he got out and bravely marched back up the walk.

"Do you know what you delivered to me?" Mrs. Ritter asked, breaking into a jolly laugh. "A toboggan! How'd you expect me to iron my clothes on a toboggan?"

Ricky was embarrassed, but he had to laugh at his mistake. He must have picked up the wrong package!

"I'll go back to the store and get your ironing board," he said.

Tinker, upon hearing of the mistake, laughed. "Why don't you deliver the toboggan anyway?" he suggested. "It goes to Mr. Kent's house. You remember him."

"Oh, yes," Pam said. "He's that nice man who's wild-life editor of the *Shoreham Eagle*." The children had had a very strange adventure in his office the summer before. "Let's take the toboggan, Rick."

Setting off again, the children delivered the ironing board to Mrs. Ritter and then drove on to the Kent house. Mrs. Kent was very happy to have the toboggan delivered so promptly, she said. Upon hearing of the school project, she gave Ricky fifty cents for the fund. As the boy was leaving, Mrs. Kent leaned down and whispered in his ear,

They set off to make the next delivery.

"The toboggan is for my son, Roger. You can keep a Christmas secret, can't you?"

"Yes," Ricky said.

"Then you won't tell him about it, will you?"

Ricky promised to keep her secret. Then he joined Pam, and they set off to make the next delivery. Several people gave money for the Christmas basket and, when all the packages were gone, Ricky found that he had $3.25. He held it carefully in the palm of his hand inside his mitten so it would not get lost.

"You did a good job," Mr. Hollister praised his son when he and Pam returned to the store. "And here's some more for my delivery boy—$1.75. Now, how much does that make in all?"

"Wow, Dad, that's five dollars!" Ricky cried.

"Right. And it will go a long way toward filling a Christmas basket."

Ricky was very happy as he and Pam started home, driving Domingo through the darkening streets. As they passed the town green, they saw a woman setting up a crèche between two little evergreens. She was arranging life-size cardboard Biblical figures in a shedlike shelter and spreading straw on the ground. The scene was beginning to look just like the manger Ricky and Pam had often seen in pictures.

"That's a fine little donkey you have there," the woman said, glancing up from her work.

"He came all the way from New Mexico," Ricky said proudly.

"I suppose you're going to enter him in the contest?" the woman asked.

"Contest?" Pam said.

Before the woman could answer, she was interrupted by a man. The Hollisters waited a few minutes, but she did not speak to them again, so they drove on.

"What do you suppose she meant, Pam?" Ricky said. "Maybe she's Y.I.F.!"

"Oh, I don't think so," his sister replied.

But to make sure, she stopped to ask another woman standing near by.

"No, that's Mrs. Morris who is fixing the crèche," she replied.

Ricky inquired if she knew about the contest, but the woman shook her head. The children went on, discussing the unsolved mystery of the burro.

"I'll bet it has something to do with the contest," Ricky declared.

After reaching home, he decided to go back to ask Mrs. Morris. So, when he had hidden the five dollars in his bureau, he hurried downtown. But the woman had left.

On the way home the boy paused to look up at the Santa Claus display on the roof of his father's store. How wonderful it looked, he thought!

After their busy day, the Hollister children went to bed early. Sometime in the middle of the night Ricky suddenly thought he was riding a fire engine. But he realized it was only a dream when he found himself sitting upright in bed. No wonder! First one siren, then another was wailing in the distance. Everyone else in the house was awakened, too.

The Santa Claus display looked wonderful.

"See how red the sky is over there!" Pam said, looking out her parents' bedroom window.

"Say, that's out in the section where the Quists live," Pete said. "I hope our Christmas tree isn't burning up. Dad, may I call police headquarters and find out?"

Getting a nod from his father, the boy hurried to the telephone on a night stand between the twin beds. The desk sergeant who answered said that Cal Newberry was not in. He was on special duty at a big fire on a farm near the edge of town.

"Is the fire on the Quist farm?" Pete asked the sergeant excitedly.

"No, it's about half a mile away," came the reply.

Pete breathed a sigh of relief and passed the good word on to the others. They watched until the glow in the sky grew less, then Mrs. Hollister said, "Well, I guess the fire's under control. Off to dreamland, all of you."

In the morning they talked again about the big blaze until the telephone interrupted them. Pete answered and found that the caller was Tinker.

"Do you want to speak to Dad?" the boy asked.

"Yes—no. You'll do, Pete. Something terrible has happened. The Santa Claus, sleigh, and all the reindeer have been stolen from the roof of *The Trading Post!*"

CHAPTER 10

The Red Yarn Clue

ALL the Hollisters cried out in dismay.

"Stolen!" Pam sobbed. "How could anyone be mean enough to steal our Santa Claus?"

"And all those nice Christmas presents in the sleigh," Holly wailed. "If Santa Claus's sleigh is gone, all the poor children's presents are, too."

"I'll hurry down and look things over," Mr. Hollister said, taking his coat out of the hall closet. "There may be some mistake."

Pete was the first to find a clue.

"Please let me go along," each child begged.

"All right. But hurry."

Everyone was in the station wagon in a few minutes, and Mr. Hollister drove quickly to *The Trading Post*. How different the roof looked completely empty! Tinker rushed out of the store to meet them, a woebegone expression on his face.

"Did you call the police?" Mr. Hollister asked, getting out of the car.

Tinker, his hands shaking with excitement, said not yet. He would do so at once.

"I can't understand why the thieves weren't seen!" Mr. Hollister said after the elderly man had gone inside. "We have such good police protection in Shoreham."

Meanwhile the children had jumped out and now started looking for telltale signs of the thieves. Pete was the first to find one.

"Dad, look at this!" the boy called from the rear of the building.

He pointed out deep tire tracks of a truck in the slushy snow. "Our truck didn't make these," he said.

"You're right, son, and no big truck came in here yesterday to make a delivery. These marks were made last night."

Pam pointed out holes in the ground where a ladder had been raised against the wall. Then Holly found part of a heavy rope which must have been used to lower the sleigh and reindeer.

Officer Cal told his story.

At that moment the sound of a siren caused the Hollisters to hurry back to the street. A squad car pulled up in front of the store and Officer Cal stepped out. With him was another policeman, whom Cal introduced as Detective Farnham.

When the policemen were told what had happened, Cal said, "All available policemen in Shoreham were called to help fight the big fire last night. This block went unpatrolled for about an hour."

"So that's when the robbery took place," Mr. Hollister said. "The thieves took advantage of the situation."

"There may even be a connection between this robbery and the fire," Detective Farnham spoke up. "Let's go to the roof and have a look for clues."

Pete and Ricky brought a ladder from the store

and the two policemen climbed up, followed by Mr. Hollister and his sons. The girls waited below.

After examining the footprints on the snowy roof, Detective Farnham said, "There are so many marks here it would be pretty hard to pick out which ones belong to the thieves. I can't find one clear set of prints."

"But the tire prints down below are," Ricky volunteered.

"Okay, son. We'll make a plaster cast of them."

The Hollisters and the policemen descended the ladder. The detective hurried to the squad car for his special kit used in taking plaster molds of tire tracks.

"We'll get a very good set of impressions," Officer Cal said as he helped pour the plaster into the deep ridges.

Ricky was particularly fascinated. "That's what I want to be someday, a policeman," he said.

"Maybe Cal will be chief by that time," Pete remarked with a grin. "Will you give Ricky a job, Cal?"

"Sure will," the officer replied. "I'll make Ricky chief of detectives." Then he became serious. Turning to Mr. Hollister, he said, "Do you suspect anybody of doing this job?"

The Hollisters looked at one another, and a queer expression came across their father's face. He did not reply, but Ricky blurted out, "I'll bet Mr. Tash did it!"

"What?" the detective cried.

Mr. Hollister spoke up quickly, explaining why his son was suspicious—that Mr. Tash had wanted their Santa Claus outfit, but added, "We're not accusing anyone. Ricky, you must be careful what you say."

Officer Cal glanced at his buddy. Then as he picked up the plaster cast of the tire track, he said, "We'll talk to Mr. Tash anyway."

The policemen drove off. But the children continued to hunt for clues.

"Better take down that ladder, boys," Mr. Hollister said, "before someone else uses it."

"Sure, Dad, right away," Pete promised.

After the brothers had put the ladder in the store and come back, Pam suddenly called out, "Look! Maybe this is a clue!"

"What is it?" Pete asked.

The girl pointed to a shred of red yarn caught on the brick wall of *The Trading Post*.

"It sure is a clue," Pete praised his sister. "One of the men who stole our Santa Claus must have been wearing a red sweater!"

Holly pulled the fuzzy piece of yarn off the wall and ran to show it to her father in the store. At that moment the police car returned. Cal pulled up at the curb and all the Hollisters went out to see what he had learned.

"Mr. Tash denies knowing anything about the

"Are you a *detective, little girl?*"

theft," he said. "Besides, he had a perfect alibi. I'm sure he's not the man we're looking for."

"I'm glad of that," Mr. Hollister said. "I'd hate to think one of our town merchants would do such a thing."

"By the way, we sent out an eight-state alarm for your missing Santa Claus," Cal said.

"What does that mean?" Ricky asked.

"It means policemen in eight states will join in the search," Cal replied.

Ricky danced up and down when he heard this. "Then our Santa Claus will be famous!" he shouted.

No sooner had the boy said this than Holly scooted off down the street like a flash!

"Where's she going?" Mr. Hollister asked in surprise, but no one could tell him.

Holly raced down the street, holding the piece of yarn in her hand. Ahead of the little girl was a husky man wearing a red turtleneck sweater!

"Wait a minute, please!" Holly called, catching up to the man.

The wearer of the red sweater turned around. He was a tall, strapping young man with a crew cut.

"You speaking to me, little girl?" he asked, smiling. "Say, you're cute. What's your name?"

Holly was somewhat taken aback by the man's friendliness. Not at all like she expected a thief to act! But she must not be fooled.

"Have you a hole in your sweater?" she asked.

The man burst out laughing. "What a strange question!" he said. "Why do you ask?"

Holly held the piece of yarn near him. It was the same shade as his sweater! She *must* learn where he had been the night before. Her heart pounding wildly, she asked, "Did you climb our roof last night?"

Again the man laughed loudly. Then he knelt down until his head was on a level with Holly's.

"Say, are you a detective?" he asked, a twinkle in his eye.

"I—I guess so," Holly replied. "But if you don't have a hole in your sweater, I guess you didn't take our Santa Claus."

It is doubtful if the man in the red sweater ever

would have understood what Holly meant had Pam
not come up just then with Officer Cal.

"Hello, Mr. Lang," the policeman said to the
man.

"You know him?" Holly asked.

"Sure. He's our high-school football coach."

Holly was dreadfully embarrassed. But Pam explained about the shred of wool she had found and
had thought might be a clue to the Santa Claus
thief.

"My sister was only trying to help," she said.

"I didn't mind a bit," Mr. Lang told her. "In
fact, I enjoyed the whole thing. But I'm sorry to
hear that the Santa Claus outfit is gone. It was a
nice exhibit."

Officer Cal had taken the piece of red yarn from

"*Don't come too close.*"

Holly's fingers. He agreed it was a good lead to find at least one of the thieves.

"I'll take this if you don't mind," he said to the Hollister girls.

"Please do," Pam agreed.

"Oh, I hope you find the mean men right away," said Holly as the officer moved off. Then she turned to Mr. Lang. "Please excuse me for stopping you."

"I'm glad you did, and good luck to you," the coach said and walked on.

Pam and Holly joined the other children and they all started for home. As they went by the little park in the center of Shoreham, Sue exclaimed, "Look, they're putting up a big Christmas tree!"

"Yes," said Pete. "That's the town tree. Let's watch."

It was the custom of the town of Shoreham each year to erect a giant Christmas tree in the center of the park. The beautiful colored lights would shine every night during the holiday season. Hundreds of visitors from miles around would come to see this and the crèche near by.

"The big hole for the tree has been dug already," Ricky remarked.

The large truck on which the tree lay had been backed onto the green. Now another truck, equipped with a tall crane, pulled in alongside it.

Four workmen attached a stout cable from the crane to the top of the tree.

Rurrr, rurrr, rurrr the crane groaned as the tree began to rise in the air. Finally the base of it slipped into the big hole.

"Don't come too close," one of the workmen warned the Hollisters and other youngsters who had gathered to watch the spectacle. "This tree won't be safely in place until the guy wires are fast."

The men drove stakes into the ground at four different points and began to attach long wires which dangled high on the trunk of the tree.

Despite the workman's warning, the crowd of children pushed closer to get a better look. The Hollisters were shoved right to the front.

Suddenly there was a loud *snap*. Everyone looked up just in time to see the cable slip off the top of the Christmas tree.

"Run, everybody!" a workman shouted.

The tree leaned over slowly. Then it began to fall toward the crowd.

Pete grabbed Sue in his arms and sped off. Ricky followed close behind, but Pam and Holly could not seem to get out of the way.

CHAPTER 11

Pete Helps a Policeman

WITH a tremendous push Pam, Holly and several other children flung themselves helter-skelter.

Swish! Down came the big Christmas tree. It hit the ground with a bang, its topmost branches stinging the youngsters as the tree brushed past. The workmen rushed forward to see if anyone had been hurt.

"We're all right," Pam assured the men.

"Thank goodness!" one of them said. "Stand way back this time," he cautioned as they prepared to raise the tree again.

The other Hollister children returned.

When the onlookers had moved far enough away, the crane operator lifted the big tree back into the hole. This time it was fastened securely.

A man raised an extension ladder up into the branches of the Christmas tree and climbed to the top. Behind him he dragged a long cord of Christmas lights which he wound among the branches. Several more strings of lights were set in place.

Then at a given signal, one of the men pulled a switch. Even in the bright sunlight the tree became ablaze with many colored lights. How pretty it looked!

It was a lovely manger.

"I never saw such a beautiful Christmas tree," said Holly. "I'm glad we came to Shoreham to live."

After the Hollisters had watched awhile, Sue became weary, and they decided to go home. As they passed the crèche, Pam looked in hopefully to see if anyone were there who could tell them about the contest. But nobody was around.

"The contest must be something about animals, since Mrs. Morris asked if we were going to put our burro in it," Pete guessed.

"Maybe it's a show," said Ricky. "I wish we could find out about it."

None of the children could figure the answer, so they walked on home. As they turned into their driveway, a great racket greeted their ears. A banging and clattering noise was coming from the garage.

"Ooh, what's that?" Sue asked, clinging to Pam.

The others started to laugh, and Ricky said, "Domingo wants a drink."

Sue was puzzled and asked what he meant. It was not until the garage door was rolled up that she found out. The burro, holding his water pail between his teeth, was banging it against the cement floor. The little girl laughed and ran over to her pet.

"That's a funny way to talk, Domingo," she said. "I'll get you some water right away, cutey-pie."

Ricky helped her, then they all went into the house. After Mrs. Hollister had heard the story of the morning's adventures and said she hoped the Santa Claus outfit would be found soon, she added, "Well, I have pleasant news to tell you."

"What is it?" the children chorused.

Then instantly Holly said, "Oh, let us guess!"

"Give me a hint," Pete begged.

Mrs. Hollister smiled. "All right. We'll have to get the guest bedroom ready right away."

"Somebody's coming!"

"That's right."

"Mr. Vega," said Sue. "He's coming to visit Domingo."

"No," her mother replied. "Guess again."

Pam's eyes glistened. "Not our cousins?"

"Yes, dear. Uncle Russ, Aunt Marge and Teddy and Jean!"

"Crickets!" Pete exclaimed. "Are Teddy and Jean out of school this early?"

His mother picked up a letter from the table and read it aloud. Mr. Hollister's brother and his family were on their way to Shoreham and would arrive the next day. The school at Crestwood, where they lived, had closed a week earlier this year.

"Will they stay over Christmas?" Ricky asked hopefully. He thought Uncle Russ, who was a cartoonist, and his wife and children about the nicest people he knew.

"I think they will stay," his mother replied. "I certainly hope so. It will make Christmas perfect!"

After lunch the girls offered to help their mother give the house a special tidying up. As on previous visits, Jean would share Pam's bed, and Teddy would sleep on a spare cot in the boys' room. They hurried off for the vacuum cleaner and dust cloths.

Since it was Ricky's turn to clean Domingo's stall, he went to do this. Pete, with nothing special to take care of, decided upon returning to *The Trading Post*. There might be some news about the missing Santa Claus outfit. When he reached the store, Pete found his father talking to Policeman Cal.

"Hello, Pete," the officer said. "I was just telling your dad we've been checking everybody we find wearing a red sweater."

They helped their mother tidy up.

"Any luck?" the boy asked hopefully.

"None. If we only had something more to work on, it would help. I was just going up to the roof to look around again."

"I'll go with you," Pete offered.

He and the officer carried the ladder outside and placed it against the rear of the building. As Pete waited for Cal to climb up, he gazed about him. His eyes suddenly fastened upon a man's rubber lying alongside a trash can. It was an unusually large, heavy one with a star imprint on the bottom. The mate was not in sight.

"Say, maybe one of the thieves lost this," Pete thought. "Nobody who works around here has a foot this large."

Grabbing the rubber, the boy scampered up the

ladder. He showed his find to the policeman, telling of his suspicions. Cal took the rubber excitedly. The next moment he leaned down and fitted it into part of a footprint.

"Pete, you've done a great piece of detective work," he said, looking up. "This kind of rubber is usually worn only by outdoor workmen. Besides, the thief who visited this roof has long feet, so he must be tall. With these clues and the one of the red sweater, we ought to be able to find him easily."

As Cal finished speaking, Ricky's head appeared over the top of the ladder. Having learned where Pete was, he had finished his job in a hurry and followed. Upon hearing the story, he cried, "Whoops! Let's hunt for the thief right away!"

The officer smiled and said this might be hard for Ricky to do. "But you boys can help me another way," he said. "Suppose you take this rubber to Detective Farnham at headquarters and tell him the whole story."

The three of them descended the ladder, and the Hollister boys raced off for headquarters. Pete carried the telltale rubber. The police station was located in one wing of the Shoreham Municipal Building, which was four blocks from *The Trading Post*.

The Hollisters ran all the way. When they arrived, out of breath, they almost bumped into a patrolman coming out the door.

The big rubber was a good clue.

"Hello, boys," he said. "Phew, you're really puffing. What have you been doing? Chasing robbers?"

"No, sir," Ricky replied, standing up very straight. "But my brother found a clue that might lead to some robbers."

In amazement the policeman listened to their story and then ushered the boys into a large room. At one end was a platform, on which stood a high desk. Behind this sat a police sergeant, answering a telephone call at a switchboard.

Hanging up, the sergeant turned to the boys and asked, smiling, "What can I do for you?"

"We'd like to see Detective Farnham," Pete replied. "We're Pete and Ricky Hollister. Officer Cal sent us with a clue to the Santa Claus that's missing from our *Trading Post*."

"Fine. That's a puzzling case," the desk sergeant said.

He picked up the phone again and spoke a few words. A minute later, Detective Farnham appeared at a side door.

When the boys showed him the latest clue, he exclaimed, "This is great! We'll keep it here for further checking. It may be the very thing that will identify one of the thieves." Then he smiled. "I hear you children have another mystery on your hands. I mean, the one about the burro. Cal tells me that every once in a while you find a note on him and you have no idea who puts it there."

"It's Y.I.F., whoever he is," said Ricky.

"Well, I'm sure you'll solve the case," the detective said as the brothers started off.

About eight o'clock that evening Holly decided to look in on Domingo before going to bed. She put on her wool cap and coat and opened the back door. As she did, the little girl noticed a mysterious shadow glide from behind the garage.

"Daddy! Come here quick!" she shouted.

As her father hurried from the living room, Holly saw a dark figure run across the yard and disappear toward the lake.

"I—I think somebody was trying to steal Domingo!" Holly cried fearfully.

"We'll see in a minute," Mr. Hollister said, grabbing a coat from a hook on the back door.

He and Holly hurried to the garage. They

found Domingo standing contentedly in his stall.

"He seems to be all right," said Mr. Hollister, reaching into his car and pulling out a flashlight. "Here, let's take a closer look, dear."

As the light shone on Domingo, Holly exclaimed, "Daddy, somebody was in here. Look!"

There was a new red ribbon around the burro's neck. To it another message had been pinned.

"Please read it, Daddy," Holly begged.

Mr. Hollister shined the light onto the paper and read,

"The time is near to play my part.
Please untie my little ——.
Y.I.F."

"Well, this is getting more mysterious every day," Mr. Hollister said as he and Holly hustled back into the house to tell the others. "And I believe you almost caught the joker."

"Oh, I wish I had, Daddy. Then we'd know what to do."

The whole family gathered in the living room to figure out the message.

"It must mean, 'Please untie my little cart,'" Pam said, "because cart rhymes with part."

Everybody agreed that this must be the missing word.

"But why should we untie the cart?" Ricky asked, wrinkling his freckled nose.

CHAPTER 12

A Mix-up

FOR nearly half an hour the Happy Hollisters tried to figure out what the note on Domingo had meant and who Y.I.F. was. They could come to no conclusion except that he probably lived in Shoreham.

"Oh, I know," Ricky giggled. "Y.I.F. means Yiminy in Forham."

"No, it's Yump in Front," Holly called out, doubling up at her own joke.

Finally Mrs. Hollister said it was high time for

"You say you have a surprise for us?"

all funny little people to be in bed, so the children went upstairs. When the older youngsters protested, Mrs. Hollister said they might talk for a while longer in their rooms.

The following day dawned clear and cold. After church services, the Hollisters ate dinner, then settled down to read. Pete had hardly finished one chapter in his book when the telephone rang. He got up to answer it.

"Uncle Russ!" Pete exclaimed. "Where are you?"

The other children gathered at the telephone and Pete repeated what their uncle was saying.

"He's only fifty miles away," Pete whispered.

Pete was silent a few moments, then he grinned. "You have a surprise for us, you say? What is it?"

Everyone waited while their brother listened. Finally he said, "Oh, please tell us what it is."

Again there was silence. Then an expression flashed across Pete's face as if someone had dropped ice water down his neck. It was followed by a broad grin.

"That's great. Wait till Dad hears this. We'll see you later. Good-by."

He hung up.

"Uncle Russ," said Pete slowly, "has a Santa Claus, sleigh, and reindeer for us."

Mr. Hollister whistled. "Our missing outfit?"

"He didn't say," Pete answered, "but it must be."

"What a cute burro."

The children danced around, asking a hundred questions. Where had he found it? How was he bringing it? In a trailer or a truck?

For the next two hours all the Hollisters waited impatiently for their relatives to arrive. Finally, just as the sun was setting and Pam was riding Domingo up and down the yard, they heard three toots of an automobile horn. A car turned into the drive.

"Here they are!" Pam shouted, sliding off the burro's back.

Pete, Ricky, Holly, and Sue raced outside to meet the visitors. As Uncle Russ stopped the car, the Hollisters realized he had not brought the Santa Claus outfit with him. After greetings were over, Ricky asked him where it was.

"Your Santa Claus and reindeer?" his good-

118

looking uncle asked. "I don't know about yours, but Aunt Marge brought one of her own."

It was the Hollisters' turn to be mystified. "What do you mean?" Ricky questioned.

"You'll soon find out, Rick. But what's this about your Santa?"

Pete quickly explained the theft from the roof of *The Trading Post*.

"I'm sorry to hear this," Uncle Russ said, opening the door and stepping out of the car. He was tall and slender and looked very much like the Happy Hollisters' daddy, though he was younger. Uncle Russ was just as full of fun as his brother. He drew comics for a newspaper strip and had a big boat, which the Shoreham Hollisters once had used on a river trip.

"It's too bad our Santa outfit is gone," he said, "but maybe Aunt Marge's surprise will cheer you all up a bit."

Aunt Marge stepped out of her side of the car, carrying a big white box. She was pretty and had a humorous twinkle in her eyes. "I'll show you what's in this box after we unpack," she promised.

As they headed for the door, Jean and Teddy spied Domingo, who had been standing patiently on the sidelines.

"Oh, what a cute burro!" Jean exclaimed, running over and stroking the animal's nose.

Jean had straight chestnut hair and dimples.

Like Pam, she loved animals and had two cocker spaniels and a pony of her own.

"Where'd you get the burro?" she asked.

Pam told her and let Jean take a short ride. Teddy came to help his sister get off and stood close to Domingo, stroking him.

Teddy was eleven, two years older than his sister. He looked something like Pete, except that he was shorter and had black hair and gray eyes.

Suddenly the boy felt a tug on his coat and looked down. The mischievous burro had torn off a button and was holding it in his mouth!

"Oh, you naughty!" Sue cried as Teddy tried to get the button back.

But Domingo would not give it up. Each child coaxed him. The little donkey kept pulling his head up as they tried to open his mouth.

"Can we eat it, Aunt Marge?"

"Please don't eat the button," Jean begged. "Mother could never match it."

"Oh, don't worry about that," said Pam. "Burros never swallow anything they shouldn't. I'll tell you what. Let's pretend we're leaving. Maybe Domingo will drop the button."

Pam was right. The instant the children started for the back porch, the burro lost his teasing look and sadly opened his mouth. His play toy fell to the ground.

Teddy dashed back and picked it up. Then Pete put Domingo in his stall and the children went into the house.

As soon as overcoats, caps, mittens, and boots had been carefully stowed away in the hall closet, Aunt Marge said, "Now for the surprise!"

She opened the big white box and lifted out a miniature Santa Claus sitting in a sleigh drawn by eight tiny reindeer.

"Oh, how pretty!" Pam said.

A hungry look came into Ricky's eyes. "Can we eat it, Aunt Marge?" he asked.

This made Jean and Teddy laugh. "You guessed it," Jean said. "Mother made this of cake and candy, but we didn't think you'd guess so soon."

"When may we eat it?" Holly asked, touching Santa's marshmallow beard with her forefinger.

"Tonight, for dessert, if you wish," Aunt Marge said, laughing. "That is, if your mother says Yes."

"Indeed, yes," Mrs. Hollister replied. "I can hardly wait to try it myself."

In a little while the Hollisters of Shoreham and the Hollisters from Crestwood were seated at the dining-room table, with the dessert as a centerpiece. Pete and Pam had inserted another leaf in the table, making it large enough for the whole group.

"Umm-yumm," Sue said when it came time for dessert. "I want to eat a reindeer's head."

Her mother said she might help herself. Sue reached over and *snap*, off came the lead deer's head. Sue held it in her chubby hand and started nibbling at the antlers.

Holly picked off Santa Claus's bag of toys, made of chocolate cake and candy. "Ummm, it's delicious," she told her aunt.

"Um, it's delicious!"

Pam ate half of Santa and Jean the other half. Ricky took the sleigh to nibble on and Pete decided on a reindeer.

This left the other animals for the grown-ups. When Mr. Hollister finished his, he declared he had enjoyed it down to the last hoof!

As they finished eating Aunt Marge's masterpiece, Pam told the visitors about their school pageant of Christmas in different lands.

Ricky said, "Our class is going to show Christmas in Norway."

"How interesting!" Aunt Marge remarked. "I was in Norway once at Christmastime."

"You were!" Pam said. "Please tell us about it."

Aunt Marge said that when she was a little girl about Pam's age, her father had gone to Norway on a business trip and had taken her with him.

"The thing I liked best about the Norwegian Christmas," she said, "was all the delicious food which the people start to make weeks before Christmas, especially the animal-shaped cookies."

"And one thing I'll never forget," Aunt Marge continued, "was that during the holidays the Norwegian children give their cattle extra food because they were in the manger on the very first Christmas Day. And besides that, the birds are remembered, too."

"You mean the birds get Christmas presents?" Holly asked.

"Good for you, Dad!"

"Yes, indeed," Aunt Marge replied. "In every Norwegian dooryard at Christmastime there stands a pole, and bound to the top of it is a sheaf of wheat. This is the birds' Christmas tree."

"Isn't that nice?" Pam said. "Do the birds come and eat the wheat?"

Aunt Marge replied that they did. The birds flocked to pick at the seeds.

"Then we ought to try it ourselves sometime," Pam replied. "Every bird and animal should enjoy Christmas."

"And *Jul-Nisse*, too," said Sue.

"Oh, you know about the little dwarfs?" Aunt Marge said. "They're cute in their red knitted caps with the hanging tassel, white coats, and red trousers."

"Did you ever see one?" Sue asked her.

"No. But I have left food. Some rice pudding." Aunt Marge's eyes twinkled. "He ate it, too!"

"Oh, I wish I could see one," Sue sighed.

During the evening Uncle Russ's family was told about the various things which had happened in Shoreham recently. Teddy was particularly interested in the mysterious notes found on Domingo. Jean wondered about the contest and also what *The Trading Post* was going to do about gifts for the poor children to take the place of the ones which had been stolen.

"I don't know," Pam said, looking at her father.

Mr. Hollister was thoughtful a few seconds, then he snapped his fingers. "If the Santa outfit isn't found by tomorrow morning, I'll put a big canvas bag in my store window and replace the stolen articles myself," he said. "Then I'll ask people to donate more gifts to the bag. We'll carry through with our project even without the sleigh and reindeer."

"Good for you, Dad!" Pam cried, hugging her father.

Soon it was bedtime and all the children were about to say good night when the telephone rang. Pete answered. The caller was Officer Cal, who said the police had picked up the first bit of evidence in the missing Santa Claus case.

"Oh, what is it?" cried Pete excitedly.

CHAPTER 13

Iceboat Detectives

"WE'VE found truck tracks on the shore of Sunfish Cove," Officer Cal said. "They match the ones we made the plaster cast of outside *The Trading Post*. Now," he continued, "we're trying to figure out why the truck went down to Pine Lake."

"Do you suppose they unloaded our Santa Claus there?" Pete suggested.

"That's what we thought at first," Cal replied. "But the question is, where did they take it and in what?"

"Boy, I wish I knew!" Pete said. "Well, give us a ring if you learn anything more, will you please?"

"I will, Pete."

The other Hollisters were eager to hear what had happened.

"There must be some good reason why the truck went down to the lake," he remarked thoughtfully. "Say, Ted, will you go somewhere with me after school tomorrow?"

"Sure. Where?"

"On Pine Lake."

Pete would not tell any more of his plan.

"I'll pick you up right after school, Ted," Pete told his cousin next morning.

"Say," Jean spoke up, "what are we going to do all day with you and Pam in school, Pete?"

When Pam heard this, her eyes sparkled. "Let's take Teddy and Jean to school with us!" she exclaimed.

Jean thought this would be great fun, but her brother said he had other plans.

"I'm going to take Domingo out for a long ride," he announced. "I'll feed him first." Teddy went outside and fed the burro. Then the boy hitched him to the cart and drove to the back porch.

"Taxi to Lincoln School," he called out as all the children but Sue came out the kitchen door.

"Goodness, can Domingo pull all of us?" Jean asked doubtfully.

"Sure," Pete answered. "He can pull over five hundred pounds."

"How many pounds do we weigh altogether?" Ricky wanted to know.

Pete figured quickly. Then he looked sheepish. "It comes to six hundred and fifty pounds. I guess we'll have to take turns."

Pam and Jean followed Holly into the cart and they drove into the street. Upon reaching the school, Teddy left them and then went on. He had gone only a block when *smack*, a hard snowball hit him on one arm.

"Taxi to Lincoln School."

Teddy looked to his left, just in time to dodge a second ball thrown hard by a boy much bigger than he. Angry, Teddy jumped to the street and ran over to the youngster, who was making another ball by packing snow around a chunk of ice.

"Cut that out!" Teddy yelled. "Want your face washed? Say, who are you, anyway?"

"Joey Brill. And I know who you are. Pete Hollister's cousin. Well, I don't like that smart guy and I don't want any of his relatives around, either."

"You talk as if you own Shoreham," Teddy said in disgust. "You stop throwing snowballs or you'll be sorry!"

A wicked gleam came into Joey's eyes. He suddenly let another snowball whiz out of his hand, aiming it directly at Domingo. It hit the little donkey on the flank with a *clunk!*

Giving a loud bray of pain, the burro jumped into the air, then tore down the street. Teddy waited only long enough to give Joey a punch that tumbled him over. Then he raced after the runaway animal.

"Whoa, Domingo! Whoa!" Teddy yelled at the top of his lungs.

The burro sped on, the cart rattling behind him, until he neared an intersection. As a car shot across in front of him, the poor animal became confused. In trying to turn, he upset the cart. The next instant the shriek of a siren frightened him still more. Domingo ran across a lawn and between two trees that grew close together.

Crunch! The burro had passed through nicely, but the overturned cart stuck fast. The wicker body, wedged between the trees, was crushed beyond repair.

Teddy, rushing up, looked at the wreck in despair. By this time several people had run to the scene.

"Was anyone hurt?" a woman asked.

"No. Only the cart." Teddy sighed. "And it doesn't even belong to me," the boy added sadly.

As he unhitched Domingo, Teddy patted the animal and said he would find him a new cart.

Crunch! The cart stuck fast!

"Maybe Uncle John can help me find a new one," Teddy thought.

He climbed on Domingo's back and rode to *The Trading Post*. Mr. Hollister was sorry to hear about the cart and immediately telephoned Mrs. Hunter, offering to pay for the wicker body she had loaned the youngsters. But she refused to accept any payment, saying she had given it to the children to play with. Furthermore, it was a very old one and of no use to her.

Mr. Hollister made two other calls. Hanging up the phone, he smiled broadly.

"It's all arranged, Teddy. We can buy a little wagon at a very reasonable price." He wrote a name and address on a paper and handed it to the boy. "Go there, Teddy, and get the wagon. It's a long narrow one with facing side seats. I'll have Indy pick up the wrecked cart."

Teddy set off, happy again. While all this was taking place, the school bell had rung. Pam and her cousin were in their cloakroom taking off their winter wraps.

"Today we're going to practice our class skit for the Christmas pageant," Pam said.

"What country did your class choose?" Jean asked.

"Italy."

Pam explained that in Italy Christmas customs are quite different from those in the United States. "Instead of Christmas trees, the people decorate their homes with beautiful flowers. A *praecipio* takes the place of the Christmas tree."

"A pr-pr— what?" Jean asked, never having heard the word before.

Pam said that a *praecipio*, found in most of the Italian homes, was a nativity scene constructed of wood, cork, plaster, papier-mâché, and other materials.

"There are angels, flocks of sheep and cattle and kings in fine, rich robes," Pam went on. "The children in our class are going to act out the parts."

Jean giggled. "You mean you're going to be a lamb or a cow?" she teased.

"Not me," said Pam, laughing. Then she heaved a deep sigh.

"What's the matter?" Jean asked.

"There's only one thing wrong with our *praecipio*," her cousin whispered, as they walked into the classroom. "Will Wilson's going to play the part of the king."

"Don't you like him?"

"He's always playing mean tricks, but we needed somebody tall to be the king."

Pam introduced her cousin to Miss Nelson.

"We're so glad to have you, dear," the teacher said. "When we rehearse our skit, perhaps you would like to help me prompt the actors."

"I'd love to, Miss Nelson."

Jean shared Pam's desk while the class studied arithmetic and geography. When the lessons were over, Miss Nelson said, "Now we'll practice the skit. Put on your costumes."

The girls hurried into the cloakroom first to do this. Jean went along. She turned to Ann Hunter. "You make a beautiful angel, Ann! Your wings look so real!"

Ann said that her father had made them. He had bent two wires and had covered them with muslin. Then her mother had sewn on the feathers.

As the girls came from the cloakroom, Will Wilson rushed toward them.

"Gangway!" he shouted, pushing his way through.

"What a rough boy!" Jean said in disgust.

The other young actors followed him. In a few minutes they returned. Will was wearing a king's costume. His robe was of red, green, blue, and white stripes, and the crown on his head sparkled with colored stones.

"Now we'll start," Miss Nelson said, as she handed Jean several sheets of paper with the different parts written on them.

The cardboard sheep and cattle were set in place. Then the live king, shepherds, and angels walked onto the scene. As they recited their lines, Jean followed each word closely.

Ann Hunter moved forward, looking very stately, her face beaming. Will approached.

Suddenly he stormed toward the shepherds and angels. The smaller children scurried to get out of his way. As Ann Hunter started to back off, Will

"Your wings look so real, Ann!"

stuck his foot behind the little angel, throwing her off balance.

Miss Nelson tried to catch the teetering girl, but Ann fell over backwards, landing on her wings. As the teacher helped her up, everyone noticed that the wings were twisted and out of shape. Tears came to the girl's eyes.

"No great harm has been done to Ann's wings," Miss Nelson said. "They can easily be twisted back into shape. But, Will, you shouldn't have done that. Apologize to Ann, and we'll go on with the play."

"I won't," the boy said defiantly, "because I didn't do anything."

"If you won't apologize," Miss Nelson replied firmly, "we won't need you in our skit. It's obvious you can't behave like a king. Someone else will take your place."

Somewhat crestfallen, Will removed his beautiful king's robe. It was given to a shorter, but better-mannered boy, and the rehearsal continued.

The children went through the entire skit, and when they had finished, Miss Nelson said, "I'm very proud of my actors and actresses."

It was time for recess, and all the Hollisters met on the playground. They noticed Teddy running toward them. He was very excited and breathlessly reported the news about the broken wicker cart and Mr. Hollister's purchase of a new wagon.

"Crickets! Now we really own something."

"Come down to the street and I'll show it to you," he said, leading the way.

The others followed and exclaimed in delight. This cart was far better than the first one they had had.

"Crickets!" Pete exclaimed admiringly. "Now we really own something! Maybe Joey did us a favor after all."

Holly hugged Domingo. "Now you look extra beautiful," she told him. "Won't you be proud to deliver all those packages on Christmas Eve?"

Domingo nodded his head, and the children giggled.

A moment later the school bell rang, and the pupils hurried back inside. For the rest of the day

Pete tried to pay strict attention to his studies, but every once in a while he would think of the sleuthing he was going to do after classes.

As soon as the final bell rang, he hurried home. Teddy was waiting for him.

"I'll tell Mother where we're going," Pete said. "Then she won't worry if we should get back late."

He found Mrs. Hollister in the living room helping Sue put on her ski suit. When Pete asked permission to take Teddy on a search for further clues, his mother gave her approval but said, "Will you take Sue down to the lake with you? She can play around with her sled while you do your detective work."

"All right, Mother."

Sue took her big brother's hand and hurried out of the house with him. The two boys ran along the shore of the lake, pulling Sue and her sled behind them. As the cousins neared Sunfish Cove, Pete said, "Watch me have some fun with this little cricket."

He pulled the sled onto the ice, ran very fast and then spun it around. Whizz! The sled turned like a pinwheel, and Sue shrieked with joy.

"Do it again!" she pleaded.

After spinning her several times more Pete said, "Will you play alone for a while, Sue?" Pete explained to her that he and Teddy wanted to look for the missing Santa Claus and sleigh.

Whizz! The sled turned like a pinwheel.

"Goodie," said Sue and pulled her sled toward a group of small children playing near by.

"We'll be right back," Pete called out as he led his cousin to the place where the truck tracks had been found. He now explained his suspicions to Teddy. "I think maybe the men who stole the outfit pulled the sleigh across the ice. There ought to be some tracks out on the lake."

"But wouldn't the police have found them?" Teddy asked.

"The men might have carried the sleigh part of the way to fool them," Pete suggested.

Walking out on the ice directly in front of the spot where the tire prints had been found, the two boys searched a hundred feet from shore. Finding none, they continued another hundred yards.

Suddenly Pete exclaimed, "Look here, Teddy!"

When his cousin reached him, Pete pointed to two ruts in the ice. "These were made by heavy sled runners," he said. "Come on, let's follow them!"

Pete glanced back to shore where Sue was busy with her little playmates. At the same time he spotted Dave Mead's iceboat skimming toward them. It stopped beside the two cousins amid a shower of ice chips from the brake.

"What are you doing out here without skates?" Dave shouted.

When Pete explained the reason, Dave said, "Hop in! We can follow the ruts much faster in the boat."

Pete introduced his cousin, and they took off. The wind billowed the sail and soon they were streaking across Pine Lake. The sled tracks were now very clear.

"Say, we're nearly to Blackberry Island," Pete said. "Maybe this is where the thieves took our stolen Santa!"

Dave came to a stop at the shore of the island.

"Look, the tracks go right up onto the island," Teddy shouted.

"Let's follow them!" Pete suggested.

Dave said he would have to stay with the boat and would wait for the boys. Pete and Teddy set off. Now they could see footprints as well as tracks in the snow.

"We're on the trail!" Pete cried eagerly.

CHAPTER 14

Overboard!

THERE was no mistaking the fact that two men, dragging a sleigh, had come to the island. Pete and Teddy followed the tracks excitedly, though a little frightened.

"We may meet the thieves any minute!" Teddy said hoarsely.

Keeping close together, the cousins followed the marks. To their dismay, the tracks and footprints went directly across the island and onto the ice again. At this point all of them vanished.

"Sue's asleep here!"

"Those men must have carried the sleigh again," Pete said in disgust. "But where to?"

He wanted to continue his sleuthing, but suddenly realized that he already had left Sue alone too long. As the two boys hurried back to the ice-boat, Pete said he would phone Officer Cal and tell him what they had discovered.

As the cousins climbed aboard Dave's boat, they told him about their latest find. His eyes lighted up. "I'll bring you fellows over here again tomorrow," he said.

"Thanks," said Pete.

As they neared the shore, Pete noticed that only a few children remained on the shore. A moment later his heart skipped a beat when he realized that all of them were older than Sue's playmates.

"I don't see my kid sister anywhere," he said to Teddy. "Her sled's still here, though."

"Why don't we see if she went home?" Teddy suggested.

"All right!" Pete agreed, but he was terribly worried.

He picked up the sled's rope, said good-by to Dave, and headed toward the Hollister house with his cousin. Bursting into the living room, he asked his mother if Sue were there.

"Why, no. Did she run away from you?"

Pete told the whole wretched story. Mrs. Hollister instantly became concerned.

"Oh, dear," she exclaimed, "where could Sue have gone?"

She called to the other children and Aunt Marge. "Has anybody seen Sue?"

Suddenly Pam remembered something and said, "I saw a box of rice cereal and an empty bottle of milk on the kitchen table a little while ago. Maybe Sue came home because she was hungry. She probably ate and then went back to the pond."

Everyone started a search which included the neighbors' houses. But still the little girl was not found.

As they stood together once more in the kitchen, Ricky suddenly snapped his finger. "I know what! Let's hunt for Sue with Zip."

The collie came bounding out to the children at the mention of his name. Holly leaned down and put her arms around the dog's neck.

"Sue's lost," she said. "Help us find her, Zip."

"Come on, Zip!" Ricky called as they hurried out the door.

The dog ran from one side of the yard to the other. Then he headed for the garage and pawed the door.

"Why didn't we think of that?" Pam said gleefully. "Sue's probably in there playing with Domingo."

But when they opened the door, the burro was alone. He turned his head questioningly at them. How they wished he could give them the answer!

The "horse's" hind foot gave Joey a kick.

Zip suddenly ran down along the shore front. The children followed as he sniffed at a set of small footprints in the patches of snow. They went all the way to Sunfish Cove.

Zip raised his head and gave several short barks. Ricky and the others could not figure out what he was trying to tell them.

"Keep on hunting!" Ricky ordered.

The dog put his nose to the ground and trotted back along the shore, then up to the house.

"Sue did come home," Pete said.

Zip nosed around the back steps, then bounded up them and scratched on the kitchen door. Mrs. Hollister opened it.

"Zip seems to think Sue's inside the house," Pete told her.

As they watched the dog, he circled the kitchen

a couple of times, then went to the foot of the hall stairway and started up.

"Zip must be off the trail," Mrs. Hollister said, "because Sue's snowsuit isn't around anywhere."

But the children followed Zip up the steps. He did not go to Sue's room, but instead whined at the door to the attic stairway. Pete opened it and clicked on the light. Everyone clomped up the steps behind the collie, with Pete in the lead.

"Sue's here!" the boy shouted in relief, running to the far corner of the big attic room.

His little sister was huddled in the corner fast asleep, her ski suit and boots still on. Sue's head was tilted to one side and her cap was half off. Beside her right hand was a bowl of rice cereal and milk.

"Sue must have been playing house," Pam remarked.

The sound of voices awakened the sleeping child. She looked up and blinked her eyes.

"Mommy, Mommy," she said, startled. "I couldn't find him, and he must be terrible hungry."

"Couldn't find whom?"

"The *Jul-Nisse!*" Sue said. "The little old man who stays in our attic at Christmas and likes rice pudding."

As the others smiled, Aunt Marge leaned down and hugged her little niece. "Bless your heart," she said. "You remembered what I told you. Well, you leave the rice pudding on Christmas Eve, and I'm sure your *Jul-Nisse* will eat it."

The whole group went down to the living room. As Sue took off her snowsuit, she told the others how she had become cold waiting for the boys.

"So I ran home to have a tea party with the *Jul-Nisse*. I had cookies, but he didn't come for his pudding."

Holly had seated herself on the floor beside Zip.

"You're a good detective dog," she said.

"You bet he is," Teddy remarked. "And your brother is a good detective, too. Pete, tell them about the clue we discovered on Blackberry Island."

Upon hearing the story, the others were amazed and agreed with Pete that he should notify Officer Cal by phone. The policeman praised the boy and

Dave guided his craft to the dock.

said he would go to Blackberry Island at once. Later that evening he called back to say there was no sign of the thieves there, though Pete had no doubt been right.

"I'm going to look some more after school to-morrow," Pete told him.

All the next day Pete was fidgety to start his sleuthing, and the time seemed to pass slowly until his teacher announced a rehearsal for her class's part in the pageant. It would illustrate a Christmas custom in Holland.

Hearing this, Pete and Dave looked at each other and grinned. They had been chosen to play the part of a white horse on which a bishop would ride. Dave would be the front legs, Pete the hind ones, with a board from one boy's shoulder to the other boy's for the bishop to ride on. A white sheet with a tail attached would be draped over them. Dave's head would fit inside the stuffed horse's head and Pete would keep his head lowered.

When the white steed was put together, Pete slumped down a little so the animal was slightly lower in the rear, and the pupils howled with laughter. Pete straightened up and the boys paraded around.

As Pete went past Joey's desk, he saw to it that the "horse's" right hind foot gave the mean boy a little kick in one shin.

"Cut that out!" Joey growled.

Reaching the front of the room, the "horse" kneeled, and the bishop, one of the smaller boys

They were hurled onto the ice.

dressed in a red velvet robe and wearing a mitred headdress, climbed up. Then a boy named Sam, who had covered his face with burnt cork, came alongside to represent the bishop's Moorish servant, Black Piet. The "horse" arose and the little procession walked back and forth.

"That's very good," said Miss Hanson, and the students clapped. "Pete and Dave, on the day of the pageant, will you please wear white trousers? We don't want our "horse" to have a white body and dark legs, do we?"

Directly after the sheet and costumes had been removed, classes were dismissed. Pete told Dave he would meet him at the dock in half an hour and hurried home. Pam said that Teddy would not be back for some time as he was downtown Christmas shopping with Aunt Marge and Jean.

"May I go with you instead, Pete?" she asked. "I'd love to help you hunt for clues."

"Come along," her brother replied.

Pam told Mrs. Hollister where they were going, then hurried down to the dock with Pete.

"It sure is blowing a gale!" Pete said, looking out across the lake. "Dave's iceboat should go like a rocket today."

"There he is now," Pam said, pointing to a speck far out on the frozen surface.

It did not take Dave long to guide his speeding craft up to the Hollisters' dock. Pete told him Teddy was not home yet and Pam would take his place. The iceboat started slowly across the lake, then rapidly gained speed.

"Crickets! We're going like lightning!" Pete exclaimed.

Dave smiled and bent forward, his right hand on the tiller. Pam grew fearful. All at once she shouted, "Look out, Dave!"

Ahead of them were several large cakes of ice which had been chopped out by some winter fishermen. Dave yanked the tiller. The left runner rose off the ice as the craft tilted dangerously.

"Hold on tight!" Pete shouted, grabbing for his sister.

But it was no use. The iceboat turned over, hurling its three riders onto the frozen surface of the lake.

CHAPTER 15

The Contest

THE three youngsters tumbled head over heels on the glassy surface of the lake. Pete, the wind knocked out of him, gasped for breath. He was the first one on his feet. Pam and Dave, however, still lay stunned on the ice.

"Pam, are you all right?" Pete cried, running over to his sister.

"Where—where am I?" the girl asked, opening her eyes.

Pete leaned down and helped her to her feet. "We were tossed out of the iceboat," he said. "Did you break any bones, Pam?"

"I guess I'm all right," Pam said shakily.

"Me, too," Dave said, limping over to the others. "Wow, that was some spill!"

The empty iceboat had skidded across the lake and now lay on its side several hundred yards away. Pete and Dave hurried over to it and flipped the craft upright.

"I'll never go that fast again," Dave said, "especially with chunks of ice lying around."

The children took their places once more, and the iceboat glided around Blackberry Island. As they neared the spot from which the thieves had left the island, Pete leaned over the side, peering at the ice intently. All of a sudden he gave a shout of glee.

"Here they are—runner tracks! This is where the thieves started dragging the sleigh again!"

Pam looked where he was pointing. Sure enough, there was a clear trail of marks, heading toward the mainland across from Shoreham.

"Let's go!" Pete cried.

But just then Dave exclaimed, "Hey! We'd better leave quick! I see Joey Brill—he's skating this way."

"Oh, dear," sighed Pam, as Dave gave the boat more sail. "I hope he hasn't found out what we're doing."

Pete glanced back and saw that Joey Brill was

There was a clear trail of marks.

skating as fast as he could after them. He was shouting, and it sounded as if he would like a ride, but the words were mostly drowned out by the whistling of the wind.

"This is one time he won't catch us," chuckled Pete. "But we'd better go a little farther."

When they had whizzed about two miles down the lake, Dave said, "Think it's safe to head back?" and, at a nod from Pete, he turned the tiller and the boat spun around.

How relieved the children were to see no sign of Joey Brill when they returned to the spot where they had picked up the trail on the mainland.

Dave followed the sleigh marks all the way to the shore. He beached the iceboat and the children got out.

"Oh, I hope we find the Santa Claus outfit," Pam said as they noticed footprints as well as the telltale tracks. They followed them over a rise of ground and into a thicket. Presently the marks zigzagged into a gully. All at once the three children stopped short. The tracks took a right angle turn into a clump of trees.

"It looks kind of spooky in there," Pam said fearfully. "Why would those men bring the sleigh to this place?"

"This is probably a short cut to the Clareton road," Dave suggested. "But we could be all wrong."

"No, we're not," said Pete, leaning down.

"Maybe someone's in there!"

Triumphantly he held up a man's heavy rubber with a star imprint on the sole of it.

"It matches the one we found at *The Trading Post!*" the boy exclaimed.

Pam looked around nervously as they continued on. Were the thieves near by? Before she could express her fears, Dave pointed a short distance ahead. The tracks ended in front of a large, dark cave.

"Maybe someone's in there," Pam whispered. "Be careful, Pete," she cautioned as her brother went ahead and looked into the mouth of the cave.

"There's a dim light inside," the boy announced.

He sniffed the air and then said, "I can smell smoke. Somebody must have a fire in there."

Pete and Dave debated whether to walk boldly into the cave or to creep in quietly.

"I think we'd better go in on our hands and knees," Pete whispered. "That way we can't be seen so well if someone's inside."

He asked Pam to act as a lookout in case anyone approached. Then he and Dave wriggled in on their stomachs.

There was not a sound from inside the cave. But as the boys advanced, the odor of smoke grew stronger. Turning a corner, they saw a reddish glow a few feet ahead.

"Embers!" Dave said. "Whoever built the fire has left though," he added, peering around in the gloom.

He picked up several dry sticks which lay near by and put them into the embers. It did not take long for the sticks to burst into flame. Immediately the interior of the cave was lighted up.

"Well, the Santa Claus outfit isn't here," Pete said in disappointment. He called to Pam. "Come on in! It's safe."

As she entered the cave, shadows danced along the black walls. Dave made torches for them by lighting sticks in the fire and together the children walked on through the cave.

It had another opening at the far end and here again were the telltale tracks and footprints.

"They couldn't have left too long ago," she said.

The three children discussed what to do next. Dave was all for following the tracks farther, so they went on. In a few minutes the searchers came

"See what I've found!"

to the Clareton highway, and here the trail ended.

"Somebody must have picked up the men and the Santa," Pete remarked. "I suggest we go home and tell Officer Cal what we found out."

The others agreed. As they retraced their steps through the cave, each child kept his eyes open for additional clues to prove, without question, that they were on the right trail.

"After all," Pam pointed out, "the lost rubber *could* belong to an innocent person."

"And the sleigh that made the tracks might not be the stolen one," Dave added.

The children again lit torches from the embers in the cave and trudged on. Dave suddenly leaned down and exclaimed joyfully, "See what I've found! Isn't this a tip off one of the reindeer's antlers?" He held it up.

"You're right!" Pete said. "Dave, you've proved this was the hide-out of the thieves!"

Excited now, the youngsters went very slowly so they would miss nothing. They had almost reached the end of the tunnel-like cave when Pam saw a tiny piece of paper almost covered by the dirt of the floor. She picked it up and after brushing it off, realized it was a newspaper clipping.

"What does it say?" Pete asked.

"I guess it's the ad Mr. Tash put in the paper for a Santa Claus outfit," she replied, "but the name's torn off."

"Maybe the thieves thought they'd sell yours to him, but didn't dare," Dave suggested.

Pam slipped the ad in her pocket and the children went on. They found nothing more and finally set off for home in the iceboat.

In the meantime the rest of the Hollister children were in the midst of some excitement of their own. They were in the living room listening to Sue. She was breathless.

"I just found another note on Domingo!" the little girl cried. "Read it to me!"

Jean took the message and said:

> "Although in Shoreham I'm a stranger,
> Please lead me to the Christmas ——.
> I promise to do my very best,
> If I'm entered in the Yule ——.
>   Y.I.F."

This poem's longer than the others," said Teddy. "Y.I.F. is getting impatient."

"Do you suppose the first missing word is *danger?*" Jean asked.

Holly shook her head. "I'll bet it's *manger*," she said.

"Could be," Teddy agreed. "Now let's figure out the next one. Something to rhyme with *best*. Zest, crest, west, test——"

Ricky gave a jump and yelled, "Yikes! I have it. *Contest!*" Then he quoted:

"Although in Shoreham I'm a stranger,
Please lead me to the Christmas manger.
I promise to do my very best,
If I'm entered in the Yule contest."

"I just found another note!"

"But what does it mean?" Jean asked, puzzled.

Ricky, Holly, and Sue were dancing a jig by this time. They explained about the crèche which had been erected near the Christmas tree on the town green.

"There must be a contest for animals to go in the crèche," said Ricky. "And Y.I.F. wants us to put Domingo in the contest!"

At this moment Mrs. Hollister came into the room. Holly quickly explained what they had discovered and said, "Please, Mother, may we put our burro in the contest?"

Mrs. Hollister nodded, and all the children quickly put on their jackets and hurried to the town green. The big tree glittered with its colored lights and a floodlight had been set up to show off the crèche.

This time Mrs. Morris was there, and Ricky asked her at once about the contest. She said a donkey, a cow, and a sheep would be needed in the manger for a few days at Christmastime.

"Of course the committee can choose only one of each kind," she said. "The decisions will be made tonight."

"Tonight!" Ricky gulped. "Are we too late?" he said woefully.

"Too late for what?" Mrs. Morris asked. Then she looked intently at Ricky. "Aren't you the boy who has the cute little burro?"

"Yes, I am."

"The winners will be notified tonight."

"And you want to enter him in the contest?"

"Oh yes. Please!"

Mrs. Morris smiled. "Put your name and address and the burro's name on this paper, please."

"May I put down my sister Sue's name?" the boy asked. "Domingo really belongs to her."

"Certainly."

When Ricky had finished he handed the paper back to Mrs. Morris and asked, "When"—he swallowed—"when will we find out if——"

Mrs. Morris smiled. "The winners will be notified tonight," she said. "I'd say about nine o'clock."

CHAPTER 16

Animal Tricks

IT WAS impossible for Mrs. Hollister to get her own children or their cousins to bed at any reasonable hour that evening. All of them except Sue talked at once and watched the clock.

Poor little Sue had propped herself up in one of the living-room chairs. She kept nodding sleepily, but would not give in to it. Every so often she would rouse and ask, "Is it nine o'clock yet?"

Someone would answer, "No. We'll tell you."

In the meantime, Pete and Pam had told of their afternoon's adventures and had phoned Officer Cal. He was amazed at their sleuthing discoveries and said the police would follow the trail where they had left off.

At quarter to nine the front doorbell rang sharply. Everyone jumped. Who could be calling at this hour?

As Pete opened the door, the others listened intently. A man's voice said, "Hello, Pete! I thought I'd drop around and talk to you about your burro."

Instantly there was a surge of children toward the hall. They were surprised to see Officer Cal,

"*You might like to have your burro perform.*"

who had stepped inside. Was he bringing news of
the contest, perhaps disappointing news?

The policeman said good evening to everyone
and then turned to Ricky. "I understand you've
taught Domingo some tricks. Is that right?"

Ricky looked startled. "Yes, I have. But how'd
you find out? I was keeping it a surprise. It was
going to be my Christmas present to the family."

"Oh, I'm sorry," the policeman said. "The laun-
dryman who comes here told me about it. There's
to be a little show given for the crippled children
at the hospital. I thought you might like to have
your burro perform."

"Yikes!" said Ricky. "That would be neat."
Then he sobered. "But when is the performance?
Maybe I couldn't do it. We're hoping——" He
glanced at the clock. It was five minutes to nine.

"We're hoping Domingo's going to be chosen for the crèche."

"I see. The show is tomorrow afternoon. I was going to ask your teacher to let you out early."

Ricky grinned. "Maybe I could do it even if Domingo is put in the crèche."

Mrs. Hollister, who had come into the hall, laid a hand on her son's shoulder. "You've taught the burro tricks?"

"Yes. And boy, is he good!" the red-haired lad bragged.

At this instant the telephone rang. All the children raced toward it, but Mrs. Hollister said she thought Sue should answer. The little girl's chubby fingers grasped the receiver.

"Hello—I'm Sue——" There was a long pause. "Oo-ee, I did? You mean, Domingo's going to be in the manger for Christmas?"

Sue was so excited she let the receiver drop and turned to her family. "We won it! We won it!"

At once there was great commotion and Mrs. Hollister had to pick up the phone to get the rest of the story. Mrs. Morris asked her if the children would bring Domingo and his warm blanket down to the crèche at five o'clock the following afternoon.

"We'll take very good care of him," she promised.

"He'll be there," Mrs. Hollister assured her. "And thank you very much. We're proud to have our little animal as part of the Christmas manger."

Meanwhile the children were clapping their hands and hugging one another. When they quieted down, Ricky told Officer Cal that he would put on the show for the crippled children before taking Domingo to the crèche.

"That's fine," the officer said, opening the door to leave. "I'll call up your principal in the morning."

The following morning Ricky's brother and sisters insisted upon seeing Domingo's tricks.

"All right," the boy said.

He took a bottle of soda pop from the refrigerator and led the way to the garage. Domingo brayed good morning and Ricky said, "Good morning, old boy. How about some tricks?" At once the burro put out his right forefoot to shake hands.

Domingo followed Ricky around.

Ricky shook it hard, then commanded, "Up, little donkey!"

The burro stood on his hind legs and followed Ricky around the garage. The other children laughed and clapped.

"Now we're going to play school, Domingo," said Ricky. Turning to his audience, he announced, "Ladies and gentlemen, this burro is very good in arithmetic. Domingo, do two and two make five?"

The little animal shook his head vigorously from side to side.

"What is the right answer? Four?" Ricky asked.

This time Domingo nodded, and the children screamed with glee. The final trick, Ricky said, would prove how extra smart their burro was. "Watch!" he told them and held the soda pop toward Domingo.

With a loud ee-aw the donkey took it in his teeth, holding the base of the bottle between his front hoofs. Then with one quick jerk he threw his head back, and the bottle cap popped off.

"Oh, he's wonderful!" Sue shouted.

Before a single drop spilled, Domingo lifted the bottle to his mouth and gulped down the soda.

"That was great!" Pete praised his brother, and Pam added, "The crippled children will love your show."

"It's the best Christmas present you could have given us, Ricky," Holly declared.

"Domingo is going to get a Christmas gift."

Late in the afternoon the Hollister children met at the town green. Ricky said that the show for the crippled children had gone off very well.

"That must have made them very happy," said Pam.

In the manger stood a small brown-and-white calf and a woolly lamb.

"Aren't they cute?" said Sue as Ricky led the burro inside. "I think Domingo's going to like them."

Mrs. Morris said she was sure all the animals would be friends. As the children stood watching, a cheery voice said, "Hello, everybody!" They turned to greet Indy.

"This is a very fine exhibit," the Indian said. "And I'm so glad Domingo won the donkey contest. By the way, I have a surprise for you. Domingo is going to get a Christmas gift."

"You mean from Santa Claus?" Sue asked.

The Indian shook his head. "From me."

"Oh, what is it?" Pam asked excitedly.

"That's a big secret," Indy said, winking.

"Oh, please tell us," Holly teased.

But the Indian shook his head No. They would have to wait until Christmas Eve, and so would Domingo. Then he said good-by and hurried off.

The Hollisters said good night to their burro and left also.

When they reached home, the children found Uncle Russ busy drawing one of his cartoon strips. It was a story of a monkey who lived in a palm tree and liked to drop coconuts on the heads of passers-by. But one day a boy climbed up and put honey all over the coconuts.

"And when Mr. Monk picked one," Ricky laughed, "he sure got into a mess."

"So he was never bad again," Sue piped. "I'm glad the boy put honey on the coc-nuts."

At supper she asked her daddy when they were going to get their Christmas tree, and Mr. Hollister said he thought it was time now to pick it up. Uncle Russ offered to take the children to Mr. Quist's directly after school the next day.

"And then we can trim it Friday!" Holly said excitedly. "That's the last day of school and we get out early."

Thursday proved to be party day at Lincoln School with the pupils in groups of twenty-five being assigned to various rooms throughout the building for fun and refreshments. The Hollisters, their cousins, and Dave Mead went to the library the last period of the afternoon

How attractively Miss Allen, the librarian, had decorated the large room! Red and white striped paper candy canes had been pasted on the windows along with little Santa Clauses and cotton snowflakes. At one end of the room stood a decorated Christmas tree.

Dave Mead had brought his accordian and he began to play Christmas carols. The children sang for a while, then enjoyed several games. Finally Miss Nelson said, "I want two volunteers to carry a big box for me."

"I'll help!" Pete offered.

"Me, too!" Teddy said.

After she had whispered instructions, Pete and Teddy went into the hall. The boys returned with a large carton, which they placed in front of the Christmas tree.

"Popcorn balls!" the pupils shouted.

The box was filled with caramel popcorn balls of all colors.

"Umm-yummy. I just can't wait to eat mine," Pam said.

Miss Allen told them that there was one for everybody and the children should line up. Pam suddenly noticed that Joey Brill and Will Wilson were in the line. She knew they had not been assigned to the library for this period and wondered if they had come just to get extra popcorn.

By this time a group of girls had linked hands and were dancing around the Christmas tree, among them Jean. When Joey and Will received their popcorn, they went to stand in a corner not far from the tree.

"I wonder what they're up to?" Pam thought, noticing their whispering and giggling.

It was not long before she found out. Joey pulled a large sticky chunk off his popcorn ball and threw it among the dancers. It landed *plop* in Jean's hair just as the school principal walked in.

"Ow!" the girl cried as she tried to remove the gooey mass from her hair.

Joey threw the sticky chunk of popcorn.

"Come here, Joey!" Mr. Russell called sternly. Joey walked up to the man, his head hanging. "Can't you behave even at a Christmas party?" the principal asked.

"We were only having fun," Joey said.

"A Christmas party is no place for rowdies," Mr. Russell scolded him. "You weren't assigned to this room. You and Will Wilson are to leave the school at once."

As Joey passed Ricky Hollister, the freckle-nosed boy made a face. "You didn't get away with it that time!" He grinned.

When the party was over, the Hollisters met Uncle Russ outside the school. Sue was with him and they all crowded into his sedan. On the floor lay a shiny hatchet, ready to be used on the Christmas spruce.

"First stop Quist's tree farm," Uncle Russ announced.

It did not take long to reach the place.

When everyone was out of the car, Holly said, "I'll show you where our special tree is, Jean and Teddy!" She dashed off and into the forest of evergreens.

"Hey, wait for us!" Pam called.

Holly was a fast runner, and the others had all they could do to keep up with her. Suddenly, the pigtailed girl stopped short and whispered in awe, "Oh, lookee, I see our stolen reindeer!"

CHAPTER 17

The Hollisters on the Stage

ALL the children rushed up to Holly, who stood gazing into the Christmas-tree woods. There in a small clearing were three beautiful deer and two fawns, their backs to the children.

"They're real live ones!" Pete said softly. "They're not our stolen reindeer, Holly."

The graceful animals stood so still, though, they did indeed look like make-believe deer.

"Aren't they pretty!" Pam whispered.

"I want them!" Sue burst out.

The sound of her high-pitched voice startled the animals. Turning their heads, they took a long look at the Hollister children. Then they loped off among the trees and disappeared.

At that moment Mr. Quist appeared. He greeted the Shoreham Hollisters, who in turn introduced Uncle Russ and their cousins.

"We came for our Christmas tree," Ricky announced.

"Help yourself," Mr. Quist said, laughing. "You know where it is."

Ricky was the first to find it. The tag bearing the Hollisters' name was still tied to the stately spruce.

168

"May I cut it down, please?" he begged his uncle.

"Sure, if you know how. Where's the hatchet, Pete?"

The older boy went back to the car for it. When he returned, Uncle Russ said, "Here, Ricky. Let's see what sort of a forester you are."

Ricky removed his right mitten and grasped the handle firmly. Then *chop, chop,* he started to cut at the base of the Christmas tree. But he was so eager to cut it down in a hurry that he chopped too fast. *Bang!* The blunt edge of the hatchet hit his knee.

"Ouch!" the boy cried, dropping the hatchet and hopping around on one leg. Then he picked up the hatchet and handed it to his brother.

"Here, Pete," he said, "you cut the rest."

Whack! Whack! Whack! The chips flew from the base of the tree, and soon Pete cried out, "T-i-m-b-e-r" so everyone would run out of the way as the tree fell. But Uncle Russ and Mr. Quist eased it onto the fluffy snow so none of the branches would be broken.

"Say, how are we going to tie the tree onto the car?" Teddy asked.

Mr. Quist said he kept some heavy twine on hand for just such situations. As he went for it, Pete, Teddy, and Uncle Russ swung the tree to the top of the car. It extended way over the back.

They swung the tree to the top of the car.

"Crickets!" Pete shouted. "This is the biggest tree we've ever had!"

When Mr. Quist returned with the strong hemp twine, Pete and Teddy lashed the tree to the roof, bringing the twine down through the windows and fastening it inside the car.

Suddenly Sue's eyes lighted up. "Oh, let's go see Mrs. Quist. She asked us to stop and visit her when we came for our tree."

Before the youngsters could dash off, Mr. Quist informed them that his wife had gone Christmas shopping and wouldn't return until suppertime. Disappointed, the Hollisters bid Mr. Quist good-by and climbed into the car. They had gone only a short distance toward Shoreham when Pam said, "I wonder why those boys back there were pointing at us?"

"And look," Pete said, "the man in the car passing us just pointed, too."

"Something must be wrong," Pam said. "Do you think the tree has come loose?"

Before they had a chance to find out they heard a loud *swoosh* and Jean shouted, "The tree fell off!"

"Oh, I hope it's not ruined," said Pam.

Uncle Russ had brought the car to a halt. Now everyone piled out to look at the precious Christmas tree which lay in the road. The boys turned it over and everyone breathed a sigh of relief. Only two small branches had been broken off. Pete and Pam carried the tree back to the car.

"This time we'll tie it on tighter," Uncle Russ said, and helped the boys fix the twine more securely. "All set?" he asked.

"Let 'er roll!" Ricky cried, and once more they started for Shoreham.

How delighted Mrs. Hollister and Aunt Marge were when the children carried the lovely Christmas tree into the house!

"Where shall we set it up?" Pam asked her mother.

Mrs. Hollister suggested they put it in one corner of the living room between two large windows.

Ricky ran to the cellar and returned with a metal base for the spruce. It did not take long for the boys to set the tree up.

"Let's trim it tonight, Mother," Pete proposed.

The "horse" did a little dance step.

Smiling, she said, "That would take too long. But suppose you put on the strings of lights now."

By the time Mr. Hollister arrived, the tree was a mass of blue, red, green, and white candle-shaped bulbs.

"It looks great," he commented.

"And tomorrow we're going to put on the angels 'n' everything," Sue told him. "But first I'm going to the school pagnet with Mommie and Aunt Marge."

The others laughed and Pam said, "It's pageant, dear."

At school next morning excitement ran high. All the pupils filed into the auditorium except the children who were to be in the different skits. The visitors sat in the rear.

The curtain rose and one after another the

classes put on their skits. How everybody clapped when Holly's class acted out scenes from Switzerland! She played the part of Lucy perfectly.

When the second-graders from Ricky's class depicted the custom of leaving food for the birds on top of a pole, there was a big surprise. Two pet parakeets pecked at the grain and then flew around the auditorium. One lighted on Sue's shoulder. She giggled in delight.

Pam's class had a beautiful nativity scene in the Italian custom, with Pam playing the part of the Madonna. This was a great thrill to her family, for she had told no one she had been awarded the part.

Pete's skit came last. What clapping and stomping of feet there was! First, a group of children dressed like those in the Netherlands came out and stuffed their wooden shoes with hay and carrots. Then they placed them beside a dish of water on the porch of their house as refreshment for the bishop's horse. When the "horse" appeared with the bishop on his back and his little Moorish boy running alongside, Sue cried out, "That's my brother in the horsie's hind legs with white pants on!"

Everyone in the auditorium howled with laughter, and the "horse" did a little dance step, nearly toppling his rider. When the curtain was finally lowered, the visitors and the pupils declared it was the finest show the school had ever put on.

The Hollisters said good-by to their teachers, and after wishing them all a merry Christmas, hurried home to finish trimming the tree. On the way they stopped to see how Domingo was.

"He's been as good as gold," Mrs. Morris said. This made the children very happy.

Upon reaching home, Pam and Jean carried the boxes of decorations from the storage room and started to open them.

"We'd better spread newspapers under the tree first," Pam suggested, "so we won't get the rug dirty."

Pete offered to go for the papers. As he picked up some old copies, the boy noticed that one was from the town of Clareton. Returning to the living room, he spread the papers out on the floor.

Teddy, meanwhile, had found a stepladder. Now everything was set for the trimming of the tree.

"First we'll put the star on top," Pam said, pulling the lovely tinseled ornament from one of the boxes. She climbed the ladder and reached up to attach the star to the tiptop of the tree.

At that moment, Holly and Ricky decided to play hide-and-seek behind the Christmas tree. Holly hid back of the spreading branches and Ricky cried out, "I see Holly, one-two-three."

The little girl dashed from the hiding place and in doing so bumped the ladder hard. It teetered.

"Oh!" Pam cried. She lost her balance and

would have fallen to the floor if Pete had not caught her.

Pam climbed the ladder again, and the star was finally attached. When she came down, Pete took her place in order to hang some brightly colored balls on the highest branches. The others began draping silver strands of tinsel on the lower limbs.

"Ummm, doesn't the tree look pretty!" Jean said.

Pete plugged in the lights, and the tree shone and sparkled.

"Mother! Uncle Russ! Aunt Marge!" Sue shouted "Come and see!"

"How perfectly lovely!" Mrs. Hollister exclaimed, hurrying in.

Some of the needles had fallen to the newspapers below the tree. As Pete started to gather them up, his eye fell upon an advertisement in the Clareton paper.

"Hey, read this!" he exclaimed excitedly.

Pam bent down to see what he was pointing at.

> **Wanted:** A large sleigh and reindeer for
> Christmas decoration. 22 Valley Street.

"Pam," Pete cried, "have you still got that clipping you picked up in the cave?"

"Yes."

Suddenly what Pete was thinking dawned on his sister, too. The crumpled ad she had found was not the one Mr. Tash had put in the *Shoreham*

Eagle at all, but a duplicate of the item in the Clareton paper!

"Oh, Pete," the girl cried, "maybe the thieves sold our Santa to these people!"

She ran to get the torn paper from her jacket pocket. It was the same ad.

"This is amazing," Uncle Russ remarked.

Mrs. Hollister and Aunt Marge nodded. The other children were too surprised to talk.

"There's just one way to find out if your hunch is right," said Uncle Russ. "We'll drive to Clareton at once."

All the children insisted upon going and hurried into their coats and caps. At the last instant Pete dashed upstairs to get the antler tip their friend Dave had found in the cave.

It took an hour to reach the outskirts of Clareton. At once Uncle Russ inquired for Valley Street. Finding it, the children began to watch eagerly. It was too dark to see house numbers but already people had turned on lights to show up their Christmas decorations.

Suddenly Ricky cried out, "There it is! I see it!"

Far back on a lawn stood a complete Santa Claus outfit which looked exactly like the one stolen from the Hollisters. Uncle Russ stopped the car.

Pete jumped to the pavement, clutching the piece of reindeer antler. "I'll find out in a minute," he called over his shoulder and dashed across the lawn.

CHAPTER 18

Y.I.F. Is Found

"It fits!" Pete cried, holding the piece of antler against one of those on the lead reindeer. "This is our outfit!"

While everyone was exclaiming, a woman came outside.

She said, "What do you mean this is yours? It is for my granddaughter who's coming to visit for Christmas."

The whole group turned. Seeing the woman's stern expression, they were a little taken aback.

But in a second Pam regained her composure and started to tell the woman why they were sure the outfit belonged to them. Just then Uncle Russ came up and introduced himself and the others. The woman said she was Mrs. Stanley.

"My brother owns *The Trading Post* in Shoreham," Uncle Russ explained.

"Oh, yes, I've been there," Mrs. Stanley said, smiling. "Please come inside and tell me the whole story."

Pete and Pam related everything that had occurred.

"You say one of the thieves was tall and the other wore a red sweater?" Mrs. Stanley asked with concern.

177

"That's what we think," Pete replied.

It was now the woman's turn to tell a surprising story. Two men, one tall, the other short, stout, and wearing a red sweater, had come to her home a few nights before saying they had read her ad in the Clareton paper and had a Santa Claus outfit to sell.

"My husband asked them to bring it right away, but the men said they couldn't until very late that night because they had to borrow a truck to deliver it in."

Mrs. Stanley gave a sad smile. "You children have convinced me that the Santa Claus outfit belongs to you. My husband and I were fooled by those men. They told us they were brothers and the decoration had been used by their family for many years."

The woman went on to say they had paid a good price, which the men insisted must be in cash, and neither Mrs. Stanley nor her husband had taken the men's name and address.

"I almost forgot," the woman said. "Those men are coming here this evening for the rest of the money! My husband wouldn't give them the whole sum because the sleigh runners were missing. They probably took them off to disguise their theft. They're bringing them tonight."

Uncle Russ stood up. "In that case, we'd better leave at once. The men may recognize us and not stop. Then they may never be caught."

Mrs. Stanley said she would call the police right away so they could take care of the capture.

"When can we take Santa?" Ricky asked.

"Tomorrow morning Indy and I will come over in your dad's truck and pick it up."

It seemed like a long ride back to Shoreham, and during every minute of the journey the children could talk of nothing else but the thieves and whether they had been caught yet. As the youngsters bounded into the house, Mr. Hollister met them with a wide grin on his face.

"Well, how are my detectives?" he asked.

"We found Santa!" Holly exclaimed.

"Yes, and you caught two thieves," her father said.

"What?" the youngsters chorused.

"When can we take Santa?"

Mr. Hollister explained that Officer Cal had just phoned. He had had a call from the Clareton police reporting the capture of the tall man who wore big, heavy rubbers and his short, stout pal who had a red sweater.

"They were captured at the Stanleys' house," he said. "The men are in jail now. Mr. and Mrs. Stanley received their money back and all the gifts that were in the sleigh have been returned."

"Everything came out fine," said Pam, her eyes sparkling. "Dad, please tell us the whole story."

He said that the thieves had admitted stealing the Santa Claus outfit while most of the Shoreham police were at the scene of the big fire on the other side of town. The pair had trucked the stolen goods to the lakeshore, piled everything into the sleigh, and taken it across the ice.

The men had hidden on Blackberry Island that night, and spent the next one in the cave on the mainland.

"They carried the sleigh part way so the tracks could not be followed," Mr. Hollister went on. "But you children were too smart for them, Officer Cal said to tell you."

The following day the Santa Claus outfit was brought back and by evening, *The Trading Post* roof glowed once more.

All the gift packages were put into the sleigh, and new ones which had been bought in the meantime were piled in behind Santa Claus.

It was Christmas Eve. Carolers could be heard singing in the frosty streets of Shoreham. *The Trading Post* was open late so that shoppers could buy last-minute gifts. Mr. Hollister announced over a loud speaker that at seven o'clock the gifts in the sleigh would be distributed.

At six-thirty Pam and Sue went to the crèche to borrow Domingo for an hour to make the deliveries.

Meanwhile, the other children had been busy. Pete and Ricky had gone home to get the cart. Teddy, Jean, and Holly were lowering the gifts from the roof of *The Trading Post* to the sidewalk in a basket on a heavy rope.

When everything was ready, Domingo was hitched up and the gifts put into the wagon. Then Pete and Sue climbed in.

Pete took the reins and away they went, with the other children running along beside them. They went from house to house. How happy all the boys and girls were to receive the gifts!

When the presents had all been given out, the Hollisters returned to the crèche. While they were taking off the burro's harness, a good-sized crowd gathered.

Among the onlookers was Indy. After Domingo had been put back in the manger, the Indian beckoned for the children to follow him.

"I have a surprise for you," he said. "Come with me."

Away they went!

As they walked toward the street, Indy pointed to his car at the curb. Hooked on behind it was the pick-up trailer which the children had borrowed to cart Domingo from the airport. Inside the trailer was a strange boxlike object.

"What is it?" Holly asked.

"Domingo's Christmas present," Indy said. "It's a portable stall. You can put it right in your garage."

"Where did you get it?" Holly asked.

Indy said he had made it himself.

"Oh, you're 'dorable!" Sue said, catching hold of the Indian's hand.

Smiling, he gazed at all the children. "Don't you know I'm your Indian friend?"

Suddenly Pam looked straight at Indy and

laughed. "I believe I've just solved the biggest mystery of all," she said, a twinkle in her eye.

"What do you mean?" he asked.

"Do you know anything about the mysterious notes we found on our burro?" she questioned him.

Indy's eyes danced, but he said nothing.

Then Pam cried, "Y.I.F. means 'Your Indian Friend,' doesn't it, Indy?"

The man laughed and said, "You're a smart girl, Pam."

"Crickets!" Pete said. "Then you're the one who tied all those notes on Domingo. But how did you attach the first note? Were you on the plane?"

The Indian chuckled. "Yes, by coincidence, I was."

"How come, Indy?" Ricky asked, realizing Indy would ordinarily be working at *The Trading Post* at that hour of the day.

"You may remember that our stock of skates, sleds, and toboggans was running very low at *The Trading Post* and your dad sent me over to Metropole Friday afternoon to pick up a rush order and bring it back with me. Saturday morning I was lucky enough to get aboard a cargo plane along with your dad's new merchandise."

"And Domingo was on the same plane?" Pam asked.

"Right again, Pam. Imagine how surprised I

was when the pilot told me the burro on board was for my friends, the Happy Hollisters."

"And that's when you got the idea for the mysterious notes?" Pete queried.

"Yes. You see out West where I come from, we always have a live burro in the Christmas crèche. I thought it would be nice to have Domingo play a part in the Shoreham crèche, but I wanted to make a riddle for you to solve."

"Boy, it sure was a hard one," Ricky laughed.

They all walked back to the manger to have a last look at the little black donkey before saying good night to him.

As they stood watching him, adoration in their eyes, Pam said softly, "This is our best Christmas ever, isn't it?"

"The very best!" the children chorused, and Domingo nodded his head.

"Ee-aw!" he said, and they were sure he was smiling. "Ee-aw!"